<u>The Fallen Trilogy:</u>

<u>Book One:</u>   Bella, A Chosen

<u>Book Two:</u>   Star Child

<u>Book Three:</u>   Spirit

Star Child

by

Diane Escoffery

Star Child©

This book is a work of fiction. All characters, organizations,
and events portrayed in this novel are either the product of the author's imagination or are used fictionally.

Characters

Ahelia...............................	Star, Star Child, Star Breath, Star Eater, Star Killer
Navarhys...........................	Spouse, Fallen Angel, A punisher
Tomas...............................	Ahelia's eldest brother
Brian................................	Ahelia's older brother
Tony.................................	Ahelia's younger brother
Paul.................................	Ahelia's younger brother
Bronn...............................	Ahelia's father
Reine...............................	Village Witch
Daniel..............................	Ahelia's tormentor
Mr. Brower........................	Brian's father
Andris..............................	Fallen Angel, an enforcer
Tahlia..............................	Ahelia's slave, friend
Xio...................................	Ahelia's slave, guard, friend
Rachel..............................	Ahelia's temporary slave
Medina.............................	Navarhys's mother-in-law
Amaz................................	Navarhys's brother-in-law
Eli...................................	Fallen Angel, Healer
Miarra..............................	Fallen Angel, Shape changer
Brahada............................	Matron in Navarhys's house
Miriam.............................	Navarhys's slave, Ahelia's helper
Tau..................................	Navarhys's slave
Prince Adir........................	Prince of Nabu
King Jenir	King of Nabu
Miriam.............................	Nursemaid
Elyan...............................	Nephilim, Child of Ahelia and Navarhys
Tau, Akim, Zek..................	Navarhys's slaves
Prince Alexander................	Prince of Lichenia
Barniursius.......................	A fallen
Maxen..............................	A fallen

All my thanks to my family

and my friends.

Chapter One

Mama tells me that I am special because on the wintery night when I was born, a star as bright as the midday sun stood over our village. People came from miles around to witness its presence. The village witch says that I am blessed because the star crumbled into a thousand silent pieces as I took my first breath. My cry, she says, could be heard throughout the hushed crowds that had gathered. Reine, the witch, calls me Star Breath. The village elder says that I am cursed for destroying God's creation. His name for me is Star Eater.

The villagers in their cups would argue one side or the other. The women, some liked me, others stayed clear, just as their children did.

I chose to believe that I was a blessing because I was the one and only girl of my parents and the middle child of five. Tomas, my eldest brother was not my father's child. His father died not too long after his birth. Brian, a year my senior, resented my very presence. Then came the twins, Paul and Tony, a year younger than me. I also thought I was a blessing because during my younger years my family, all but Brian, treated me so special.

My legal name also given to me by Reine, is Ahelia. She tells me that it means 'breath' in a foreign tongue. When I could sneak away from home as a child, her house was one of my favorite places to visit. I loved how colorful her home was. How her home smelled of all different types of plants and herbs. In the winter her fireplace kept her home warm. She was full of stories and good advice. Outside my parents, she was the only other adult whose advice I treasured.

"You are the breath of a star Little Sis," Tomas would tell me on the nights we would sneak out together. Tomas, eight years my senior, told me this all during our years that we lived together. "Let the villagers say what they want, I witnessed a miracle."

Brian did not get along with Tomas either. Their disagreement had something to do with the land the family farmed. Our farm was big enough to feed our family and supply our village with a variety of eggs, vegetables, fruits, and on occasion meat.

We all helped on the farm. I helped less than the boys because mama needed me also. Mama and I kept the house clean, the family fed, and the clothes clean and mended.

Mama handled the money. Not many knew, Daddy did not do well with figures. I attended our little village school more than my brothers. Mom made sure that I went, as she had done in her younger days. We were unlike most families who insisted the boys go and the girls stay home. My brothers attended when the work lessened on the farm. As a result, I was more advanced in my studies than my brothers. One more reason for Brian to hate me. He felt that he should have been picked to attend the most, but our father needed his help.

My father had a sparkle in his eye just because of me, his only girl. When I was little, he sometimes would give me a ride on his shoulders. I loved his attention. We sometimes went into the village to deliver surplus or to get supplies. He taught me how to ride a horse and how to steer a wagon.

In all these things I was lucky, and I revel in them all. My luck ran out in my tenth year. A donkey kicked me and knocked me senseless.

I lay unconscious for almost two full weeks with my left leg and a few broken ribs. In that world between the living and death, I met someone. He was tall, dark and extremely good looking.   He stood like a giant, sporting broad muscular shoulders, a trim flat stomach, and well-defined legs. His dark hair fell in waves just below his shoulders. In my dream, the sun glistened off his caramel skin. But what really spoke to me was his piercing eyes. At first, I could not tell the color, but they fit him well.

In that place of nothing, he came to me. "Star Child, I will come for you." He bowed, then came closer. I could now see his eyes. In my dream, his eyes looked the same color as the late evening summer sun. He leaned down and kissed me on my cheek.   He whispered in my ear, "Wake up and fight!" Forces pulled us apart and then he was gone. The image of him burned in my memory like a brand on a beast.

Opening my eyes, I wished for death. I found that my chest and part of my abdomen had been wrapped tightly. My broken ribs hollered and echoed throughout my body. I lay burdened with an uncomfortable splinter on my left leg. The construction of that splinter consisted of four slim boards also wrapped with torn clothing. I labored for every breath that I took. My leg felt like a heavy painful burden. Every slight movement I made was a journey of torture.

My one comfort, in those dark days of my recovery, was that I could feel him. I felt his presence every minute of each day. I could not explain it to anyone. I knew that I felt what he felt. I felt his everything and wondered if he felt me. Did he know how badly I hurt? If he did, why did he not come? I knew he was real. That he was not just a dream that is slowly becoming a part of me.

My parents and Tomas took turns sitting with me, but I was not in the mood for company. Just them talking felt painful. Tomas was the only one who tolerated me and put me firmly in my place. I confided to him that I feared that I would not be able to ever walk again. He scolded me, saying that I was being foolish.

Just as Tomas finally got around to telling me what had happened to me, a braying rose from the direction of the village.

"What is that?" I asked Tomas, for he sat keeping my company.

"I do not know, but it sounds like an animal in pain." The sound was not loud where we were but enough to gain our attention.

"I hope it is the donkey that kicked me."

It was that donkey.

Villagers who were there playing cards saw the donkey drop awkwardly. When they checked, all the donkey's ribs were broken and all four of its legs.

The donkey suffered from the same injuries that I had, but to a more serious degree. The way the beast collapsed did not make sense with the seriousness of its injuries. All the villagers had to listen to the animals agonizing cries. The donkey's owner had to wait for Mr. Peter, the blacksmith, to return home so that he could borrow his gun to end the donkey's misery. The animal suffered and had attracted a crowd. This latest incident did not sit well with the villagers.

Reine visited and refused to be put off by my moodiness. I told her about my gold eyed stranger, and she smiled, "Ahelia, this man you speak of, will bring out your greatness."

"How do you know that?"

"Have I ever told you lies?"

"No." Everything Reine tells me is true. "Does my savior know that I am in desperate need of him?"

Reine laughed her musical laugh. "You will find that you will always be in desperate need of him. You will crave him like you crave the air that you breathe." I sat awkwardly on the floor, where my brother Tomas had gently placed me. He had propped me up alongside Reine. She whispered in my ear, "Daniel will be like a plague upon your soul. Try your very best not to hurt him."

Daniel was a bully at my school. I turned to look at her. "Why do you tell me this?"

"You know Star, if you do not, you suspect." *'You believed I hurt that donkey.'* I felt betrayed and glared at her angrily.

"I more than believe it, I know it." She looked at me with seriousness.

I smiled. I had not stated my thoughts, but she answered. It was like that with her. She hid it from the others, but with me she did not bother.

"You are rising, Ahelia."

The village vicar returned to my home on the following day. They tell me that he had given me last rites as both Tomas and my father bandaged me up.

"I have come to see how you are doing, Ahelia." The vicar says, smiling in his fake friendly manner.

"Why trouble yourself, I do not attend church?"

"Ahelia!" My mother reprimanded me. "Mind your manners!"

Still, in a lot of pain, I was not particularly in a mood for visitors. I had been rather sharp with the few persons that had visited. If he was waiting for an apology, he would be waiting a long time.

"Did you hear the braying of the donkey last evening, Ahelia?"

I did not want to answer.

"Ahelia, the vicar is asking you a question," my mother added sternly.

"I thought he had come to see how I was doing," I responded as if it was just her and I.

He shifted uncomfortably in his seat then turned to speak to my mother. "The townsfolk think there is witchery amongst them.   They think your daughter is a….", he lowered his voice, "…witch."

My mother inhaled audibly.

"They think I killed that donkey?" I asked pointedly through my extreme discomfort.

He turned towards me, "They think you had something to do with the beast's injuries."

"I am in misery, in this bed because I was kicked by a donkey. How could I hurt a soul in the condition that I am in?"

"The same donkey that kicked you was the one that was injured then killed. I doubt they think you did injury to the beast physically."

"You came to see if I am a witch?"

He nodded, "It is just…"

"If I was, Reine would have taken me into her confidence a long time ago."

"She is not a witch of sorts; she is a healer. They are not accusing you of being like her." To my ears, his voice sounded ominous.

"Do you think I am a witch, Vicar?"

He looked at me, bandaged and helpless. "I think we are all children of the Lord."

"I am tired mother. I don't want any more visitors from this Vicar or anyone else." I turned my head away from them both and closed my eyes. I worried about what they were saying about me. At that moment I recalled that the donkey started braying the moment my brother informed me of how I got hurt. *'Was Reine right? Could I have really done what they suspected?'* Witches got burned at the stake. I had to be careful or else they would burn me. As my heart thumped at my rib cage and fear settled in my gut, I vowed that I would heed Reine's warning. I would swallow my anger if I could help it.

"Your leg is mending Star Breath." Tomas would tell me and reassure me that I was getting better.

Tomas began helping me to walk after two months abed. I was so weak; my father fashioned a crutch for me to lean against. My left leg did not heal the way it should have. A malformed knot remained in my shin and my leg remained weak. I mourned my loss freedom this would impose on me. Life became far worse than I could imagine it would.

The other kids made my life unbearable both at home and at school. I could no longer run and play with them. I missed running with them, swimming nude at the slow-moving river in the summertime, climbing the nearby rocky hills and exploring our underground caves. I missed my freedom. More of them started calling me Star Eater. I could not do the little farm work that had been my chores. My brothers had to do more chores because I could not. Brian and the twins resented me. I still helped mom in the home and attended school when Tomas could get the horse and cart to take me there. Unfortunately, I took time out of his work, but Tomas had faith in me, more than I had in myself. The worse was my father. He stopped being the loving father I needed. He no longer spoke of me with pride, and he avoided me when he could.

I told Tomas about the stranger in my dreams. He looked at me with big brown loving eyes. "I hope he will do for you that which I cannot." I felt his admiration.

When I told my other family members about my stranger, they laughed. Believe me or not, I could feel my stranger deep in my bones, within my person.

Brian's scorn of me deepened. Tomas, Mama, and Reine were the only people in this world who took an interest in me. For them, I am eternally grateful.

At our school, a room inside our church, in the middle of the village, Daniel, the school bully, made me his special target. He called me Star Eater before the incident. Afterward he referred to me as 'The Cripple.' He would ape the way I walked. He would kick my crutch away from me and hide it until I cried. Once, after school let out, he kicked me on my bad leg. I fell to the ground clutching my leg and crying for someone to help me. I bawled unhindered by the way I appeared, afraid to think of Daniel while the embers of agony shot through my leg. All of the village children stood around unsure whether they feared him or feared me more. None helped me. When Tomas arrived to get me, he got Daniel to get my crutch which he had taken again. Tomas beat him bloody in front of me and made sure everyone knew he would give anyone else the same should they bother me in the future.

Tomas's threats did not deter Daniel. In class, he would move my chair from under me as I tried to sit. He would throw my chalk, break my chalkboard, rip my shirt and constantly call me names. The other kids called me names also, but none were as nasty and spiteful as Daniel.

At the age of twelve, I stopped going to school. I stayed home cooking, cleaning, mending clothes and feeding our animals. Brian replaced Daniel in torturing me. He called me names, created unnecessary messes for me to clean, complained to father about me, and got me into trouble whenever he could. Many times, when one or both the twins did something wrong, he would turn the event around and place the blame on me. He put a dead squirrel in my bed as I slept. I woke feeling the furry sticky thing under my covers. I almost died from fright trying to get away from it. Brian and the twins thought it was funny. Tomas did not.

Tomas, being almost as big as my father, Bronn, began to whip the boys, starting with Brian. Bronn came to the rescue of his sons and demanded that Tomas stop.

"Boys will have their fun. No need to beat them."

"Fun? Ahelia is hurt because of their funning."

"They didn't mean to hurt her."

"They are hurting her always and you do nothing."

"It is time for her to marry."

"Are you mad? She is still a child!" Tomas yelled his outrage.

Smiling smugly my father replied, "I have an offer."

Marching up to his step-father Tomas bellowed, "I will not allow you to rid yourself of her." He spun to look at our mother, "Mama say something!"

"She is too young Bronn." My mother with tears in her eyes looked at me sadly.

"No one will want her with that...that deformed leg." Bronn twisted his mouth while pointing at my disfigured limb.

Angry that I disgusted him, I spoke up in my own defense. "Someone will want me, and he is coming."

"There she goes with her tall tales again." Paul stuck his tongue out at me, grateful his father came and stopped Tomas's assault.

"He will come!" I barked at them. I had the dreams more frequently now and still sensed his presence.

Tomas managed to put papa's plans to marry me off until I turned fourteen. At that age, most of the village girls were married. Only Tara, who was simple, Marna, who was ugly and me, the cripple, were still single. Tara would never get married, at eight and twenty she was considered an old lady. Marna stood a chance though she was twenty. She could cook, clean and make clothes. Me, I still waited for the man in my dreams.

Then one night I dreamed of the orange-yellowy eyes of my man again. He told me to run. I guess he did not know that I could not. I woke to find Daniel sitting at our table with his father, Lester.

Papa for once welcomed me with a smile, "Come Ahelia, it is time."

I hobbled over to where he sat. "Time for what papa?" I approached apprehensively. I did not like this, but a small part of me liked that he was being pleasant.

"For you to have your own family."

I looked hatefully at Daniel. His smile was one of evil triumph.

"I have my own family here." My heart began to thunder within me.

"The Browers have come with an offer."

"Refuse it," Tomas demanded overhearing my father's words. "They come here because Mr. Brower no longer has a wife. It is no secret that he battered his late wife and treated her like a servant. Now they need a replacement. Daniel made Ahelia's life hell while they went to school. He would not be a good husband for her. No one else in the village wants their daughter married into that family. So, he comes here."

"Ahelia will never marry if she refuses this offer."

My stomach knotted, "I will marry, but I will not marry him."

"The agreement is already made."

"I will not do it!" Rising from my seat, I turned, tripped and fell almost on my face.

Tomas came to my rescue. He gently picked me up. "See he laughs," he motioned his head towards Daniel. "He did not even try to help Ahelia. I will not have her marry him."

Bronn stood outraged, "She is my daughter and I will have the last word in this matter."

Tomas held me and faced him. "This is my land. I support her. I support the lot of you. I say she remains a maiden until I see fit." Tomas hardly ever stated his claim to the land his father left him. "I will do for her so that she does not burden you."

Silence.

My father looked on embarrassed and angry.

He turned and took me to Sally our only horse, a nag really. He placed me on Sally and then he placed the reins on her.

Whispering, though no one could hear us, I asked, "What are you doing?"

He placed his fingers on his lips, "We are leaving."

"To go where?" I had not been off the farm in eons.

"To the village witch. She warned me about father's intentions and told me to take you to her." I then told him about my dream the night before.

At Reine's house on the far side of the village, she stood at her doorway and welcomed us.

"You will not be here long. They will come to force your hand." She smiled worriedly towards me.

"Tell us where we must go."

"Head west. The one you dream off, Star Breath, is on his quest to find you."

She hurried out the front door, untied our nag and slapped her rump. Sally scurried out towards the dale. Reine turned to Tomas, go quickly to Peter's."

"The blacksmith?"

Reine nodded, "He will supply you with horses."

We headed west. We both rode steeds. My left leg did not like it on a horse, but through the pain, I continued towards my destiny.

Reine told us that we would meet the one from my dreams two days ride west. We rode as hard as I could go. That night we rested near the crest of a hill overlooking a river. The witch had given Tomas smoked pork, cheese, and wine. Usually, children drank wine only during the festival at the end of our harvest. Tonight, he gave me a small bladder full and told me to sip it, not drink it down quickly.

"It may lessen the pain you feel in your leg."

"What about the one in my back?" I teased, though I meant it.

He held his flagon up to the sky and added, "This one is for you, the pain in my arse."

We laughed together.

"Look at that star Tommie," I pointed to the brightest star in the skies. Tommie looked, he knew what my next question would be, "Was my star brighter than that one?"

"Star Breath, your star was as bright as the midday sun and much closer. I sat on the roof of our house because I had to look straight up at it. I was a wee lad of eight, and I had just heard the story of the Christian king. Your star exploded quietly as I heard your first cries. I heard Bronn say, 'It's a girl.' I stood up and hollered his same words to the crowds that had gathered about our farm. They all kneeled and called you a miracle."

I loved my brother. He always told the same story differently. It always left me with a warm grateful feeling inside my belly.

Tommie and I set off early the next morning. My leg, at first, felt numb but then pain crept in and grew intensely. I bravely bared it to get where I needed to go.

We saw them from our viewpoint on a ridge. I knew he was among them. My heart thundered in my ears. The convoy kicked up dust on the plains and we could not tell if they were soldiers or not.

We reached the base of the ridge by midafternoon. By that time the convoy had started to make camp near a small brook that ran the course of the plateau.

As Tomas and I approached, a small party of five broke away from the camp and started to ride towards us.

He rode at the head of the party on a grand stallion as black as a starless night. He looked tall even on his steed. His cloak made of tanned hide and sable fell in ripples down almost to the stirrups. His wavy dark brown hair fell just below his shoulders. He sported a light mustache and a tapered black beard. His skin was the color of wet sand that I had seen in pictures painted of beaches.

My stranger dismounted almost before his horse stopped. He walked with purpose to where I sat on my horse, put his hand out, beckoning to me. I looked into his unusual eyes and momentarily, the world fell away.

Though in my heart I wanted to go to him, my leg pained me badly. I could not accomplish the movement to dismount. As an explanation I uttered, "I cannot. My leg."

He reached up towards me with both hands held out expectantly. I leaned over towards him like a trusting child. I looked into those orange-yellowy eyes as he caught me and placed me on the ground in front of him.

Tomas liked his show of chivalry.

He stood tall, a head and shoulders over me. His shoulders were broad. His face looked just as it did in my dreams. I could not take my eyes off him. He stared right back at me, with his hands still under my arms. "You are the vision in my dreams."

"As are you," I replied with a smile.

He pulled me into his embrace. "You are tired." Not a question but said as a statement.

"Yes," I replied simply.

"Will you journey alongside me?

"Yes."

"Will you keep yourself beholden to me?

"Yes."

He looked into my eyes, "Will you obey me?"

"Yes."

He turned to go, but I tripped. He looked down at my misshapen leg. "I will fix your leg after we marry." He gently and effortlessly picked me up.

"You fix legs?" I asked while comfortably entrenched in his arms; not feeling the least bit awkward.

"I fix anything, once it comes to you."

Though I did not know if he spoke the truth, I took a measure of comfort from his words. In his arms, all my pains vanished. I felt great. "Fix it now," I uttered barely above a whisper. Not sure if I should be demanding of his services so eagerly. He may think I challenged his truthfulness.

"So, you can run from me?" He smiled down at me and I noted crow's feet next to his eyes. His breath smelled of something spicy and sweet and I felt hard muscles beneath his clothing.

"Fix my leg and you will have to be the one running from me. I would be your second shadow."

His stomach jumped as he laughed, showing beautiful straight white teeth.

"What is your name?" I smiled pleased that I made him laugh.

"My name is Navarhys."

"Na...va...ris," I pronounced slowly.

"Na...var...hys," he corrected.

He placed me on his horse and mounted behind me. Navarhys put his right arm across my abdomen and guided his horse over to Tomas. "Is he your brother?" His voice took on a deepening tone that resounded within me.

"Yes Navarhys, this is Tomas, my eldest brother."

"Then, you are my brother also." He reached over and shook Tomas's hand. "Navarhys, pleased to make your acquaintance."

"Tomas." They shook hands. "Pleased to meet you too, Sir."

"Will you trust me with your sister's life?"

Tommie looked at his sister's hopeful eyes. "Is he the one, Star?"

"He is the one."

Tomas looked at him a while, taking in his measure. "Yes. I will trust you with my sister's life." They shook hands again.

"Come rest with us." Navarhys turned his stallion towards his camp. The four mounted men with him allowed him to pass them to lead the way back.

A huge campfire lay at the center of camp with a forest dear roasting above it. The armed men numbered twelve, with just as many ordinary folks. Four ordinary wagons made up the caravan along with a few erected tents.

Navarhys carried me to one of the tents and laid me on skins beside another woman who slept soundly.

As the sun began to set, I woke alone. The rumble of men's voices and their laughter felt welcoming to me.   Whatever it was that they were speaking about they were having a very good laugh.   As I walked up to the group, I saw Navarhys explaining something to Tommie.

Tommie excused himself. "You are awake, Star." Tomas smiled turning towards me.

I smiled hobbling toward him. Around my brother, I was not ashamed of my bad leg. At that moment I did not have the benefit of my cane. Tomas came to me, picked me up and placed me beside Navarhys, around the fire. I felt Navarhys's stare even when I was not looking towards him. The varied food was bountiful that night and I again sipped on wine.

Navarhys would not hear any of Tomas's objections, I was to lay with him. He welcomed Tomas to lay near us. Tomas did.

The next day we headed east, towards my village because Navarhys wanted to obtain my father's consent. This made me extremely nervous. Tommie explained the circumstances by which we left, but Navarhys still insisted that we return and get the consent. Again, I rode with Navarhys on his horse. At least while riding with Navarhys, I felt no pain. I loved the feel of his body near mine and its warmth.

Chapter Two

On horseback, sheltered within his cloak, he began to tell me our story. I listened intently, as we journeyed back towards the village of my birth.

He started with the words that would define my existence, "You are my chosen."

"Chosen? By whom?"

"The creator."

"What does it mean, 'chosen'?"

"We share one soul, you and I." He paused and I felt him warming, as did I. "Does it not feel intoxicating to be near me?"

"Oh yes, it does." My every fiber felt invigorated. I felt as if I could run the length of my village. I did not even feel the pain or even an ache in my leg as we rode together.

"I feel the same." He kissed me just behind my ear. "We cannot help it. We are destined to be together." He rode on in silence for a little while then he added, "The star that bought you, took my beloved."

I turned suddenly in the saddle to look up at him, but he looked away. I felt his loss.

"I am sorry."

"She was beautiful, carefree, and... she was mine."

He fell silent once more. I felt his hurt as if it was my own and did not like it.

"How did you meet?" I asked trying to get his mind away from the death of his beloved.

He smiled; I felt it. "I was out hunting with my riders when we came upon them at the roadside."

"Them?"

"Aeyden and her mother. Aeyden lay dying, very close to death. Her body broken by the wheels of a Vardo. Her gypsy clan saw that caring for her would be hopeless. They chose to leave her behind. Rawnie, her mother, stayed behind with her to ease her passing.

"When Rawnie saw me, she knew me."

"Like how I know you?"

"No not like you."

"How so?" I turned again to look up at him.

His sand-colored eyes peered down at me. "I am a fallen," he stated.

"A fallen?"

"…Angel."

I did not laugh or find it funny. "Like in the Christian stories."

"Yes." His breath felt warm on my ear.   "Rawnie begged me to fix her daughter. She threw herself on the ground before me and promised she would be in my service for life and that I could have her daughter for myself if only I would save her. Right in front of her mother, I mended Aeyden's body. Though Aeyden was a true free spirit, she honored her mother's wishes and she became my lover. I fell deeply in love with her. I loved her so badly, I wondered if her mother had placed a spell on me. Aeyden, being a free spirit thought me confining. I was, but I only sought to protect her. Rawnie returned to her clan, but I insisted that Aeyden stay with me. The following winter when Aeyden knew her people would be returning, she begged me to allow her to go see them. I refused; they had left her to die. Her mother had an open invitation to visit us. Aeyden was unhappy with my decision. She stopped speaking to me and I stubbornly would not relent." He sighed deeply. "I had an occasion to attend, with a few business acquaintances. I ordered two of my slaves to watch her. She slipped away during the night. She intended to make it back home before I returned the next morning. I found her dead on the side of the same road from which I had saved her the year before. Three gypsies and Rawnie were with her, preparing her for burial. I ripped her from them. Her devastated mother told me that she knew our time together would have been short-lived. "Death, she said, "...refused to be cheated." Her mother asked me if I saw the bright star the night before. I informed her that the star was meant for me. Rawnie told me that she knew that too. That you had been born the instant my beloved Aeyden had died.

I turned towards him as much as I could in the saddle, wanting to look into his strange eyes. "What killed her?"

His deep hurt increased the longer he looked down at me. I saw the scene as he saw it. The responding ache in my heart showed on my face. "Do not tell me anymore," I begged, very upset. I dreamed of this man since my misery began, only to find that he loved a ghost. I wanted him to love me.

"I will," he whispered gently.

'Are you answering my thoughts?'

Gently he answered, "Yes, I am,"

He hugged me tighter. *'You are destined to be mine.'* He had not moved his lips and I read his thoughts. I could not read Reine's thoughts although she read mine on many occasions. Then he kissed me on my cheek. I felt our bodies heat as one.

I slept against him that night feeling gloriously at peace.

We reached the village before noon the next day. Navarhys ordered his fighters and the rest of the contingent to make camp near the village, near Reine's home. After the camp was settled, Navarhys's top riders rode with us heading to Tomas's farm.

Word of the camp must have gotten to My father. He and seven villagers rode mounts coming towards us, as Navarhys with me on his horse, Tomas and the soldiers rode towards the farm.

"Thank you, *Stranger*, for bringing home my runaway daughter." My father looked at me riding together with Navarhys with nervous eyes. "My name is Bronn, father to Ahelia." He dismounted.

"Stay," Navarhys whispered in my ear. He dismounted and approached my father. The mounted villagers, which included Mr. Brower and Brian, faced us just as the soldiers, Tomas and I faced them from behind Navarhys. My father also dismounted.

"Navarhys Xander." He shook my father's hand looking into his eyes. "I have come to broker an agreement of marriage to your daughter."

My father looked toward at me on top of Navarhys's horse. I saw it in his eyes, he could not believe it; all that I had been saying was true. "My house is yours. Your men may find rest where they can for it is not a grand house."

I smiled triumphantly over at Brian. He returned an angry look.

That night as I sat next to Navarhys, I watched him repay Brian's father his bride price, then pay my father in gold, horses, and iron for my hand.

My mother made ready my bed and another for Navarhys in our main room, but Navarhys insisted that I lay with him in his tent.

Outside a big tent had been erected for Navarhys and I. Inside the tent a pallet of skins, candles and an old man with very close-cut red hair awaited us.

Navarhys informed me that the red-headed man was a slave and a scribe. Slavery in Lichenia had long been abandoned. In my village, I had never seen one. I thought maybe they looked different from regular people, shorter or maybe deformed. The old scribe began to write the marriage contract as Navarhys dictated.

In the morning, Navarhys took me to the river that partially ran through Tomas's land. There we bathed together. Navarhys made sure that I did not stumble. Tomas got clothes for me but struggled to find clothes big enough for Navarhys to wear. He need not have worried, Navarhys's slaves brought clothes from his wagons from the other side of the village. He dressed in a brown pair of trousers, a long white shirt, and a long brown leather jacket.

I dressed in a simple dress of the palest blue, the length down to my ankles. The village vicar, my family, and a few villagers came to witness Navarhys and I say our vows: "To love, honor and cherish for an eternity."

My heart thumped throughout my body when our lips touched. It was not fear, but the anticipation of new beginnings. I welcomed it all, with a hope that I thought that I had lost.

Navarhys gave my brother two of his male slaves to help him with his farm, and an equal share of four horses that he had given to my father. Additionally, Tomas received gold, spices, fabrics, and many skins. More riches than Tomas would have seen in a lifetime. Their transactions were conducted in private. My husband also left four of his men, skilled freemen, at Tomas's command.

Navarhys's bride gift to me was a beautiful black mare. Though her head was black, she bore white speckled spots on her body. I named her Galaxy because she reminded me of the night sky. I loved her immediately. Despite my lame leg and the ache that would follow, I rode her through the surrounding fields. Tomas was busy with his new charges and Navarhys allowed me to ride out alone. I had not moved about so much in a very long time and relished my newfound freedom. I enjoyed the air as it wisps past my face and blew through my loosen hair. Riding Galaxy was untethered freedom. I rode her anywhere I wanted.   My father's riding lessons, given to me long ago, returned to me as if engrained. Upon my return, I saw in his eyes and the smile that played on his lips, that Navarhys loved that I was happy.

He helped me off my horse and relieved me of my aches. "Go with your mother, she wants to help you pack."

I smiled happy to do as he says.

While my mother and I were packing, I felt a sharp cutting pain in my shoulder. It hurt worse than my leg that had begun to ache again. I had to sit down and rest as my breathing became labored.

"What is wrong, Star?" Mom asked as she came to sit next to me, very concerned.

I lay within her embrace, shaking my head as I explained my newest affliction. My skin seemed unbroken. To ease my aches mom, got water from our well, wet cloths and placed them on me. This treatment helped my leg, but I still felt the shearing pain in my shoulder.

My younger brother, Tony, came running into my room, without a knock. "Your husband has been shot, Ahelia." At least he had the decency to look alarmed.

I lost the little coloring I had. "What?" This could not be. My stomach felt like it would drop from my body. I knew instinctively that it was Navarhys's pain that I felt.

Brian stuck his head around the door an evil smile played on his lips. "Your foreigner is asking to see you before he dies."

My worries clouded my mind. "What should I do?" I asked looking up at my mother. My heart twisted because life seemed so unfair. Like a constant seesaw.

"Ahelia, go to him, quickly." She stated urgently, helping me to my feet and feeling for my crutch.

With my mother's help, I hobbled out to my horse. The two riders left behind to assist me had my horse saddled at the ready. One helped me to mount, while the other held Galaxy still. Off we galloped to the other campsite.

"Come quickly Star Breath. He needs you." Reine beckoned to us, as she stood just outside of her cottage. One of Navarhys's riders helped me dismount.

His entourage including my brother stepped aside so that I could shuffle in. Navarhys did not look like himself. His skin had changed to the color of a ripened tomato and his eyes were now a reddish-brown. He lay on a pallet in the witch's house with a deep hole in his left shoulder. On the floor beside him lay a bloody arrow.

Navarhys put his right arm out to me. I hobbled toward him without hesitation. "Lay with me."

I did as he bade, hugging him as tightly as he hugged me.

"I am sorry!" I cried, knowing somehow this was all because of me.

"Do not worry, Wife." His voice, rich but unearthly. "Everything will be fixed."

I placed my hand on his cheek. Though he did not sweat, his skin felt hot to my touch. As I looked on, his skin temperature returned to normal, his eyes became their brilliant orange-yellow and his skin return to the color of the late afternoon sun. I looked at his shoulder. It had not a blemish. The deep wound that had existed in his shoulder before I lay down with him and my corresponding pain, both gone.

"Now it is your turn." He let me go and rose. My brother, the villagers, and I seemed surprised by this incredible event. He issued orders to one of his men in a foreign tongue. That man stepped forward and held my shoulder down onto the pallet.

I looked up at the soldier and then at Navarhys, alarmed. "What are you doing?"

He smiled slightly, then answered, "Mending your leg." He pulled my skirt up around my waist. "It will hurt, Wife. Bite down on this." He took his belt off and handed it to me. I took the strap from him, putting it in my mouth, my tongue held below its musty taste. Navarhys turned to my brother and ordered him to hold down my right leg.

The pain as he twisted and rubbed my left shin, was as if he had broken it with an ax. I screamed like I was being murdered, then blacked out.

When I came to my senses, Navarhys laid next to me. He held me in his arms. I now felt no pain. I felt like I was floating in a warm mist.

Looking into his eyes, I saw the reflection of candles in them. "Is it over?"

He nodded once, "You are fixed."

I smiled cautiously looking down at my left leg. Sitting up looking incredulously at my straightened limb. I ran my hands down its length. Standing timidly, I bounced on my legs. Took one step, no pain. Another, then another. A flood gate of tears blinded my vision. I turned to Navarhys and threw my arms around him. Sobbing my gratefulness.

'You will not have to worry about me leaving you.'

"Why not, you can run now?" He whispered gently in my ear.

He read my thoughts again. I smiled, embarrassed. I caught sight of my brother. He had tears streaming down his cheeks. I went to him and hugged him too.

"I could not have done that for you."

"Tommie," I smiled putting him at arms distance. "...because of you, all this has happened."

I felt Navarhys pull me back toward the pallet. He placed me to sit there. "Do not move from here." His eyes changed first to a darkened burgundy.

"Jun Balka Tay!" *[Hold them!]*

The six villagers; my father, my twin brothers, a visitor to our village the Reverent Tallow, Vicar Derby and Tomas, whom all were already frightened by what they saw, found themselves restrained against their will. Reine remained at liberty and looked on seemingly unaffected. I, who have known them all my life, said nothing, though my heart beat almost painfully in my chest.

I watched Navarhys change. He grew another two feet, his skin darkened to blood red, his facial feature became more pronounced and bigger, and his fingernails and teeth lengthened. My family and the villagers cried for mercy.

Navarhys walked slowly over to the visiting Reverent. On his way over to him, Navarhys bit into his left middle finger. The reverent, recited what I came to know as 'The Lord's Prayer'. Navarhys targeted his heart. He sank his sharpened hard talon slowly into him, along with half his injured finger.

"What are you doing in this village Reverent?"

"I come because we got word that a man of wealth has married here."

"Who is we?"

"The Church at Broxhall."

"Who told you?"

"The crown's spy."

"What is his name?"

"Sir Walter Cooke."

Navarhys then proceeded over the town vicar that married us the day before, listening as that man rebuked him as Satan. He poked his bloody finger into the vicar's heart unceremoniously.

The twins, Paul and Tony, were next. They were held together. Their cries fed off one another. Navarhys bit into his index finger on his other hand and took the twins together.

They screamed right until the end. I pitied them but watched fascinated at the peaceful look that came after their terror.

"You will not ever disrespect your sister, not even for a moment."

He then turned and walked up to Tommie.

"Star! Stop him!" Tommie cried struggling in the arms of two of Navarhys's guards.

I wished that I could, but Navarhys looked at me sharply, baring his teeth.

Tears sprung to my eyes. I did not want Tomas hurt, but I was not frightened. I sensed the fear in my beloved brother and hurt for him. Navarhys quickly shoved his injured finger into Tommie's belly. I wanted to scream, but the thought of doing so remained a thought. I looked on knowing somehow that the ends justified the means. Tommie would be forever changed, but it would be better for us. Tommie's cries died down. A look of peace came over him. I was glad that his suffering was short-lived.

"For treating my chosen like a princess, you will forever be my brother."

He left my father for last. His cries were pitiful. My heart thumped for him. "You, I will not consider my father. A true man looks out for his family, no matter the sickness or injury. No matter the financial loss."

"I did not think she would have another chance to marry. I did not wish her ill."

With that, he bit into my father's arm.

I looked away.

'You had better look this way Wife! We are one soul. What I do, you do.'

I heard his thoughts. I looked back and saw my father trembling in the grip of the fangs of my husband. I looked at them and did not breathe until Navarhys released him.

He came to me changing slowly back to his human form. Navarhys held my hand, I felt him drawing energy from me, replenishing his own. I saw his fingers heal. He kissed me on my left cheek. I felt how pleased he was with me.

"You did not run."

"I gave you my word." We smiled towards each other.

My father, the villages, his men and Reine kneeled before us as one looking at Navarhys.

"Now we go to get vengeance," Navarhys stated, donning his bloodied tunic.

Tomas asked, "On who?"

"Come, Brother," Navarhys stated authoritatively, "… and you will see."

Tomas's heart quickened within him. I felt it pounding.

I turned to see Navarhys's eyes had turned to that reddish-brown color.

Though he spoke in a foreign tongue, I knew what he said when he ordered the two soldiers to return me to my mother. He wanted me, returned to my mother and no-one else. "Guard them!" he ordered in English. His tone gave no room for dissent.

I returned home on my horse Galaxy, not the least troubled by the recent occurrence. Everyone seemed at peace.

Hearing our horses, my mother and Brian waited just outside our farmhouse.

I dismounted and walked towards them seeing the shock on their faces.

"You walk straight?" My mother worded in total shock.

I smiled proudly. "Navarhys has healed me and I healed him." I looked at the disbelief on Brian's face and enjoyed the mixture of envy and contempt I saw there.

"He has given me that horse also. Her name is Galaxy." I had not told them earlier because Brian was not home. I turned towards my horse. "Isn't she a beautiful horse?" She was. Her black coat was sprinkled with white spots, just like stars.

Brian disappeared into the house as I neared our mother.

Mom and I went to my small room. She had been very busy packing my small case with my treasures from my bottom drawer and with other items she thought maybe I would need. I had no idea what my new home would look like. I could only imagine that it was big. Mama advised me in the ways of a woman. A milestone that I had not reached yet. What I would expect while carrying babies and during childbirth. She made it all sound scary but something that I would have to tolerate. I listened attentively, wanting to experience it all with Navarhys.

That night my husband did not come back to me. I slept in my bedroom. I dreamed of Navarhys and I woke with a smile on my lips.

I woke up to the rumble of activity outside my window. I looked and saw that Navarhys had moved his caravan to the farm. I hurriedly dressed, gobbled breakfast and ran out to see what was happening up close.

While the soldiers divided the equipment needed for those being left behind, the slaves helped to pack food from Tomas's land, weapons and equipment onto the wagons. Navarhys left a few pigeons behind also.

My husband, I saw, was busy but I wanted to know what had transpired last evening.

Tomas approached me first. "Sis, you are looking rested and well." He kissed me on my cheek.

"You do too Tommie." I laced my arm into his. "What happened last night?" I leaned into him.

"Navarhys will inform you."

"Come Tommie." I pleaded, pulling him closer. "I will not tell," I whispered playfully.

"No, you wait!"

I looked at him. Tommie rarely, if ever, raised his voice to me. We were always sharing our secrets. I pulled my arm out of his angrily, turned and began to walk away.

"Sis," he caught me by my shoulder. "I am sorry." He pulled me into an embrace. "Things have changed. I cannot tell you what he has forbidden."

I looked into Tommie's brown eyes. He was still my brother, but different. I now sensed the change deep inside him.

"Wife!" Navarhys strode towards us. He came, held my hand and kissed my cheek. "Come."

I smiled holding his hand. We spoke of pleasantries until we were seated on a fallen log. The brook ran soothingly nearby. Navarhys wanted to know how I was treated by everyone.

"Why?" I asked shyly, not wanting to relive a painful past.

"I have become aware of some things."

Once I began to speak, I could not stop. I held nothing back. Afterward, he held me as I cried. My feelings of hurt, still fresh as the words.

"Please do not cry, Wife. After this day, no one in this village will ever think to trouble you. His eyes darkened.

We walked holding hands to Tomas's barn. Inside both, Brian and Daniel hung strung up by the arms, from the rafters, naked. Navarhys's men and slaves were all there, Reine and a few family friends from the village.

I averted my eyes.

"No Wife," he moved my head to look in their direction. "Know that they are nothing and cannot do anything more to harm you."

I looked at Daniel first. I saw the deep hatred he had of me.

"Daniel you may now apologize to my wife for all your wrongs towards her." Navarhys pushed me towards my nemesis. I did not want to go but I did. I moved slowly towards him. A hush fell over the crowd gathered.

As I neared him, he spat on me. "You are still a deformed bitch."

Navarhys flashed by me. He punched Daniel so hard, teeth, blood, spit, flew from his mouth and blood flew from his nose. I stepped away hoping none of Daniel's blood got on me.

From in the back, I heard a smothered cry. Turning I saw Lester, Daniel's father, tied to a pole. I had not noticed him before.

My husband issued a command in a foreign tongue. A soldier moved towards Daniel then punched him hard in his belly.

"Apologize!" Navarhys demanded.

"I a… sor…"

"Louder," shouted the soldier on his right.

"I un sorry!"

"Wife, what do you feel about that apology?"

I looked at Daniel, a faint smile on my lips. His face looked awful. Resentment still lingered in his eyes. "He is saying what must be said. His heart does not share the words of his tongue."

In a foreign tongue again, he issued another order. I watched as one soldier lower him to almost touching the ground, the other bought our barn stool near Daniel. Navarhys grabbed Daniel's left leg and held it on top of the stool.

Navarhys then positioned me to stand directly in front of Daniel. Navarhys stood beside me.

"Daniel is your name! My wife says you lie. You are not truly sorry, but even if she forgave you, I could not. For your attempt on my life." As quickly as he said it, Navarhys lifted his left hand and came down on Daniel's left leg, breaking it so badly, his knee looked bent backward.

Daniel could not manage a scream. His eyes rolled to the back of his head. Sweat poured from him. They cut him down and released his muzzled father.

"Now Daniel will forever know what my wife went through, and you Lester will have to cater to your selfish son and taste what he has been doing to others around him."

"He is a good boy!" Lester managed through his tears.

Navarhys darkened. "You think I do not know that you plotted with him." Navarhys smiled over to me with his darkened reddish-brown eyes. "They wanted to kill me, then return to have you married to Brian."

Mr. Brower paled.

Navarhys turned his attention to Brian. "Now you!."

"I am sorry Ahelia. I am sorry I caused you any suffering. I am sorry." His apology could be heard clearly. Fear resided in his eyes which darted between Navarhys and me.

"No," Navarhys shook his head. "You must list your transgressions."

"I do not remember them all."

"List them backward... to the best of your ability."

Brian looked uncomfortable and frightened. "I am sorry I told you that your husband was dying."

"That is not the last transgression. The last one!"

Brian looked around wildly. "Papa, stop him!"

I looked back and saw my father stand without expression retraining my mother as guards with weapons drawn, stood by them. I felt the change in my father that I had felt earlier in Tommie.

"My last time for this request. Your last transgression?"

"I... am...I do not remember."

"You do not remember killing Galaxy?"

"My horse?" I could not believe it. I saw the truth in the fear perched on his face.

I do not remember moving towards the boy that was no longer my brother. I delivered a blow with my right hand to his cheek. It felt like I had hit a piece of stone. "I will always hate you." His cheek turned gray.

Navarhys pulled me away. He turned to the gathering. He changed before all those in attendance. His tan foreign features now looked red. He now looked like a red human. His face, full of muscles creating deep lines.   He growled, bared his sharpened teeth and he grew in height, two more feet.

"Let it be known, that if my wife is offended, so will I be." His men knelt noticed a few from the village followed suit bowing their heads.

Navarhys touched Brian on his arm. Brian cried out, witnessing his arm turning the same grey color as his left cheek and his fingers twisting. "Now you will look at your face and know your sister hates you and you will look at that hand that took away her property."

"No please, she can have the horse my father gave to me."

"You mean I should take back one of the horses I gave to him?"

"Please! I will do anything."

Navarhys melted back into his human form. He whispered in my ear. "Let us ready for our meal, we leave in the morning."

Before dinner, I found myself in my bedroom with my mother. "Isn't it exciting mother?"

She nodded. "Aren't you frightened?"

"I am excited." I smiled.

"Frightened of him?"

I looked at her. "Navarhys?"

She nodded worriedly, wringing her hands together.

"He will protect me."

"What if you anger him? He is not like an ordinary man."

"He is my fate, Mama. Whatever he is, he is mine and I belong to him." I did not want her to remember Navarhys in his other form. I stroked her hair and wished that the memory be gone. I sensed the moment the memory evaporated, and I looked at her face and saw her worry being replaced with happiness for me. I had successfully pulled the memory of Navarhys's change from her thoughts. This discovery was like opening an unexpected present. I smiled with my mother happy for us both. Now I thought of the other people in the village who had also seen his change and were probably speaking of it. I wanted the memory dropped from them also. I saw their faces in my mind's eye and sensed that I had accomplished that also. I did not want them speaking of the event. I wonder what other gifts I had.

That night I said my goodbyes to my family. Brian was not among them. He bemoaned his disfigured face and crippled arm and stayed out of sight. My family joined the camp and ate out in the open camp under the stars.

I sat between Tommie and Navarhys. I sensed Tommie's sadness. I was sad that I was leaving him but very excited to be leaving this village and its divided people.

"Look at that star Tommie," I said pointing to the only star out that night.

"It is a beauty, is it not?" Navarhys stated not knowing our game.

"Was my star brighter than that one, Tommie?"

"No star was ever as bright as the star you were born under. Your star was so mighty it turned night to day.

"Your star took the life of my Aeyden."

We both looked at him. Navarhys looked lonely, hurt and lost.

"But it gave you a miracle, my sister," Tommie stated firmly.

Navarhys looked at me sadly. I held his hand. He was still grieving. After all that time, he still yearned for her.

"I am sorry Navarhys."

We lay together in the great tent that night. His presence made me feel so wonderful. "Do you know how good I feel laying with you?" I asked him, wondering if I was already in love with him.

"Yes."

I looked into his eyes. "Please do not hate me."

"I do not hate you."

"You blame me for Aeyden's death. I feel it."

"It was my fault. I should have heeded my call, but I chose to ignore it."

"Your call?"

"That star beckoned to me for three nights. I refused to acknowledge it. Usually, a star like that is only visible to the one fallen it was meant for. It became visible to humans because I would not follow. That way tales of your birth could reach me, and I would still find you."

"Will you love me?"

He pulled me closer to him. "Let's rest. We start early tomorrow." Both of us still dressed, he pulled me towards him and covered us with his clock.

Early the next day my parents came to our tent to bid us a final farewell. Navarhys and I lay talking about his home.

"Good morning Navarhys, morning Ahelia."

We both looked towards them entering our tent.

"You are up early." I smiled shyly turning toward them.

"We came to wish you both a safe journey."

"And to see if I am a monster," Navarhys added shortly.

I turned to Navarhys with knitted brows. He pulled his cloak from about me. "See she is still a child. Better than how she would have fared with Daniel."

My father reddened. "I did not believe in her dreams. I only wanted her to have a husband.

Navarhys rose. "Understandable." He kissed me on my cheek, greeted my parents and departed to start preparations to return to his home.

"I now know that Daniel was not the best choice and I ..."

"I have already forgiven you, Papa." I went to him and hugged him. "Navarhys will be a good husband and provider. Do not trouble yourself over me."

"Will I ever see you again?" My mama wailed. "Hardly anyone leaves this village why must you go?" We embraced tightly. My heart ached for us both. I know I would surely miss her.

"I am special Mama. I always have been.

Chapter Three

The journey to the docks took us three days of hard travel. In the meantime, we were being followed. Navarhys order two of his trusted riders to capture the spy. They did. He was one of the King of Lichenia's men of ranking.   Not surprisingly, Navarhys's large party did not land in Lichenia without notice. There had been a spy on his tail since.

"I meant no trouble," Navarhys stated. "I came to take my wife home with me." He took hold of my hand.

"She is a farm girl, is she not?" The spy asked revealing his gathered knowledge.

"Where I am from…," Navarhys turned from his neutral position facing the fire, towards the spy, "…a man does not inquire about another man's wife?"

"I meant no disrespect." I sensed the gentleman's heart rate increase and saw sweat form on his brow. Though I could not see Navarhys's face, I knew he was showing his anger. "I see how well-heeled you seem to be and…"

"Tell your sire, I was just here to claim my wife."

Navarhys did not want or need to continue this conversation and abruptly ordered two of his men to escort the spy back to his horse. Navarhys rose and followed behind. Soon afterward, I heard a blood-curdling scream.   A while later Navarhys and his men reappeared.

"What happened?"

"I sent Sir Walter Cooke on his way with a story and a heavy satchel of gold." He smiled with me. I looked into his eyes and knew that he had also made that man an ally.

Navarhys's ship took us by sea five days south. I enjoyed my time at sea as a new adventure except for a spat of seasickness that I experienced on the second day at sea. I was only allowed on deck early in the morning when most of the crew on the ship were still asleep or late in the evening as the sun settled and Navarhys had time to be with me. Otherwise, I was tucked away in our cabin. It was nothing grand. A small porthole provided the only light. A desk, a table with a map on it, three chairs and a narrow bed. The nights were peaceful and quieter than farm nights. I lay nestled with Navarhys, sheltered within his arms. It felt like heaven.

The Kingdom city of Nabu, my new home, sat on a port. It seemed to rise out of the sea as we neared it. Nabu covered two rocky mounds and beyond. Six other ships of different make and sizes, sat within this city's large port. I looked on in awe at this place that seemed like a dream. The first thing about this new place that I liked was its warm weather.

Four people came to greet us. Shadiya, introduced to me as his slave of many years. Shadiya bore the same complexion as Navarhys. Her dark brown hair was cropped very close to her scalp, though she was beautiful still. She wore burgundy lip stick, her eyes were lined with black markings to give them a more dominant appearance. Her clothes were clean, flowing, and stylish. I looked at Navarhys and he looked at me with his sand-colored eyes.

'I know what she is.'

He read my mind. 'She is what I tell you she is.' I sense the scolding from his thoughts.

He introduced me to Brahada, the matron of his home, then to Andris, his assistant. Lastly, he introduced me to Rawnie.

"You are Aeyden's mother?"

"Yes, Star Child. I am." She smiled sweetly, pulling me discreetly away from Navarhys.

He sensed it and looked over to us. "Rawnie, that is far enough." I felt embarrassed seeing the alarmed look on Shadiya's face and an air of look of aloofness on Brahada's. Navarhys resumed speaking to Andris, but I knew he kept his awareness of me.

"I had to meet with you. Since you know who I am, I will assume that you know about my daughter's death and your birth?"

I nodded twice.

"I just had to see if...maybe her spirit is reborn in you."

She stopped us and turned me towards her, gripping my hands firmly so that she could get a really good look at me. She slowly turned and began walking again. "You are not her. You are you. My daughter is gone."

I felt badly for her loss; a mother outliving her only child. My heart ached in sympathy.

Just then we noticed the group stopped. All had turned back to look at us. Andris's eyes were that dark reddish-brown I have seen on my husband. The others had their look of disappointment.

"Come, walk ahead of us!" Navarhys ordered angrily.

We walked between them, then few steps ahead.

Rawnie spoke again, 'You doubt his love for you."

I did not reply. I thought I would not like to discuss this with her, a total stranger.

"I was the one who insisted that it was time to bring you home."

I looked at her with renewed interest. I thought of all that time that I waited for him. Rawnie had been that push to get him to get me.

"His long neglect of his duty could not continue. You were getting of an age to be a wife."

"He can't touch me anyway."

"I was not concerned about Navarhys, I was concerned about you being someone else's bride."

"Oh."

"He deeply mourns my Aeyden."

I nodded.

"But you are here, and you must make him know it." She stopped and made me look at her, "Understand?"

I nodded, still unsure but answered, "Yes."

The city looked to be made of sand. Many of its homes were built of adobe brick and sandstone. Its inhabitants were of many different skin shades and wore colorful garments. Slavery was a part of the way the city operated. Then there was a servant class and a professional class. The city's outer walls were as thick as an average size man and its outer door made of tree trunks.

Rawnie excused herself and left with Shadiya as we walked through the market.

My love held my hand tight enough so that I knew not to stray. Everything I saw amazed me. The constant rushing of people from one place to another. The intermingling of carts, people, horses, dogs, cats, and the scurrying of smaller creatures.

Tommie was left a relatively rich man, but I wondered if he would have liked it here.

Andris hired an open carriage for us. Navarhys sat beside his assistant and continue their talk. I sat alongside Brahada. She did not speak to me, nor did she look in my direction. She sat ramrod straight throughout our journey. To me she seemed afraid to enjoy the comforts of the stuffed backed seats. I didn't pay her much mind. Looking at the different sites, the various people, crowded and unfamiliar streets, elaborate houses and the small plain huts, poor people, and people of substance. It all was so fascinating. I later learned that Navarhys had purposely taken us around Nabu, so that I could see the many places that I saw.

Navarhys's home, like many in his area of the city, was gated and had tall outer walls. Inside those walls stood a beautifully manicured garden. As we entered his gate, I saw the path that led right up to the house. The carriage veered off to the left wrapping around the back of his home. Here stood a small stable, a second outer detached building and a sandy old patch of earth. The house did not appear to be as big as I had imagined it. Like the other homes, it was mostly the color of sand. The structure stood two stories high. Its windows and the door at the front looked cut out of the walls. The big wooden front door stood out black and shiny.

Navarhys introduced me to staffers that past us, as, "My wife, Ahelia."

This home had many rooms on its first floor. It was much bigger on the inside than it appeared from outside.

The second floor housed, among others, mine and Navarhys's adjacent bedrooms. I realized after he opened my door to show me around my room, that he meant for us to sleep in separate rooms.

"Navarhys, could we not lay together like we have been doing?"

"No!" he stormed. "You will sleep in this room. I will have your possessions sent up to you."

"Why can we not lay together?"

He looked back at me. "You are still a child."

"But we…"

"You will sleep in your own bed." He moved towards me with darkened eyes causing my heartbeat to quicken.

"Your wish, Navarhys." I was very disappointed. I loved laying sheltered in his arms. It made me feel so very good and safe. *'Loved'*.

"I want you to remain inside the home until I secure a handmaiden and a guard for you. This can be a very dangerous city.

"As you wish Navarhys." But I was confused, "Where are your men?" I was sure he could have someone from the soldiers protect me.

"They were hired and dismissed upon my return."

"The slaves?"

"Leases. Less affluent families will lease their slaves. I don't like for mine to travel."

He smiled and kissed me on my cheek. Pleased, I too smiled, before he turned leaving through our adjacent door.

Not too long after, I heard a knocking at hallway door.

"Come in!" I called as I sat looking out my window facing the beautifully manicured front garden. This whole place was like a dream. The house was on a bit of a hill so I could see part of the plaza beyond our wall. Children and grown-ups congregated there.

In came an older woman and a man, older than Tomas but not as old as Navarhys. I greeted them the way I heard they do here when speaking English. I stood facing them both. "Welcome."

"Welcome wife of Navarhys. I am Medina, wife to the late master of this house."

We held hands and kissed each other's cheeks as part of the cultural greeting.

"This is my son, Amaz. Son to the late master of this home."

"You mean step-son," I corrected. Navarhys spoke of them during our time spend together.

"Ah, he has told you of us," She nodded with a knitted brow.

I nodded once. Amaz, a good-looking man, had dark straight hair pulled back into a tail at his nape. He had light brown eyes like his mother and a light brown complexion like her also. He sported a goatee similar to Navarhys. Maybe, that was the fashion here.

"Did he tell you that my late husband is not his true sire?" Medina persisted.

"He told me many things; that among them," I answered feeling her slight.

She looked caught off balance by my words. I wondered if she knew that I was aware that her ungrateful son warred with my husband over this house and her late husband's businesses.

"You seem very young."

I did not like her emphasis on the word, 'very', and took offense to it. "I take close care of myself."

"What are you doing here?" Navarhys shouted entering my room through our shared door.

We turned to see Navarhys's rage printed on his face.

"I am accompanied!" Amaz stated equally as loud.

"Get out! You are not welcomed in this room." Navarhys proceeded to stalk over to Amaz, grab him roughly by his shoulder and dragged him abruptly towards the exit, then he shoved Amaz out the door and slammed it.

He turned to address my other *guest*. "Medina, I will not tolerate you side-stepping my authority. By my honor to my father, I may have to abide your presence, but Amaz will have to find his own way if I believe he is trying to get close to my wife."

Navarhys turned to me, "Wife, come."

He led me through our connecting door to his bedroom. His quarters were grander than mine. His chamber held a bathtub crafted from wood. Carved into the side of it were numerous positions of joining between a man and a woman. The wooden bathtub in my bedroom was plain. Our canopied beds bore different color curtains. His with white silken curtains and sheets, mine with lavender and pink. He had beautiful skins on his bed of animals I have only read about. His floor covered partially in rugs. His room had windows facing the same city plaza as mine but also another one facing the thicket of trees on the side of our home. He had a trunk with his clothes just under the window which I was sure doubled as a bench. An oversized desk with one chair beside that. Another two chairs sat beside his bed and a stuffed long chair along one wall. Unlit candles hung on sconces from the walls.

"What do you think?"

"Of what?" There were so many things I had seen.

He smiled, "Of everything!" he held my left hand within both of his.

"Everything is grand. I have never been to a city. Everything is so close, and everyone is so busy. I cannot believe so many people live in one place. How do you get to know all their names?"

Navarhys laughed a jovial belly laugh. I loved how he sounded. "One does not know everyone. You know some by name, some you know their faces, others are just people you greet just because they are passing by."

Astonished I asked, "No one is angered by you not addressing them properly?" In the village, children had to properly address those older or else when your parents found out, you would get a sound thrashing.

"Some. You will get to know that." He reached behind his back on the overstuffed chair that we sat on, then presented me with a thick gold chain and two matching bracelets. "You must wear these at all times." He placed the jewelry on my wrists and the chain around my neck.

"Thank you Navarhys." I looked into his beautiful eyes and smiled.

He apologized, "I am sorry I was short with you earlier."

I nodded holding up my bracelets for closer inspection. They were each fashioned after a rope with the clasp looking like links in a chain. "What does it mean?"

"It means that you are taken." He turned me to face him. "I cannot lay with you here." He continued, "There are many perils on a journey that do not exist here. This district is gated within a gated city. Only the wealthy and their slaves live within these gates. He reached for my hand and looked into my eyes. "I had to keep you safe."

"I just feel so… '*loved*' …safe when we are together."

"You are safe here. You are still young and not familiar with the ways of a man. Some perils also exist here." His whole body deepened in color. "We wait for you to mature." The kiss he gave me then, tingled to the far reaches in my toes.

Two slaves bought our food. I now knew how to distinguish the slaves. Their heads, men and women, were shaved. Navarhys ordered the woman slave, Sytha, to taste my food.

"Does your '*slave*' live in this house also?"

Navarhys darkened again. "No, she lives elsewhere."

"Why?"

"You ask too many questions. Return to your own room."

"Navarhys introduced me to Tahlia, my handmaiden. She was a slave, my own age. Tahlia was a beautiful brown tone with dark wavy long hair. Her father owned her mother. Recently her father died. To hear Tahlia tell it, 'Her *father's wife could not wait to sell* her *mother to someone and* Tahlia *to anyone else'*.   Tahlia unlike some slaves was recognized by her father and would have been freed upon her maturity. Now that Navarhys is her new master, he did not have to honor her father's wishes.

"Why is your hair not cut?" I asked her.

"Slave children's hair are left alone until they mature. In the plaza, you will see slave children and the children of the master's play together."

"Strange."

"Not at all. Adult slaves run away; most times, children stay with their parents."

The handmaiden and I decided to run around the gardens to explore. The front garden was a beauty to behold. Grass, flowers, and edges lined up as if commanded to do so. A grand fountain in the form of an angel stood in the center of the garden. Paved walkways also in straight lines. I had never seen nature behave so.

"Mistress, that is not nature. People plant them that way," Tahlia pointed out to me.

"But eventually the plants will do what they do naturally?" I thought to myself, after all, it was not like they were planting crops.

"Mistress, people prevent them from growing wildly."

We walked and talked of plants as we proceeded to the sparse woods at the side of the house. Just beyond the tree line, we met Medina and her son Amaz.

I spoke first, "Greetings, Medina. Greetings, Amaz.".

They greeted me, "Greetings wife of Navarhys."

"You look splendid this fine day," Amaz spoke moving towards me with his handsome smile.

I took one step back. His aura did not agree with me. "Likewise." I turned slightly looking at Medina. "You also look gracious, Medina."

"Thank you."

Just then Amaz grabbed my arm and pulled me towards him. "Do you not know that it is dangerous walking around without an escort?"

I stared at his hand on my arm offensively. "Do you not know..." I looked into his brown eyes, "...that you are lucky that I am in a good mood."

He released me, smiling nervously. I saw him for what he is, a little boy standing in his mother's shadow.

"Navarhys will not want you out in the gardens. You should return to the house where it is safer," Medina offered cordially.

"Thank you for your advice," I commented a little worried. I decided to do just that.

We were in the den later drinking tea, when Amaz told on me. "I found your wife wondering alone outside today."

Navarhys stormed over to me and grabbed my hand. He saw all.

Though I made no mention of it, he spun on Amaz. "Why did you put your hands on my wife, Amaz?"

Amaz looked at us strangely. "I...I was trying to impress on her how dangerous walking out alone could be."

He stormed over to Amaz, towering over him by at least a foot. "If you touch her again, I will cause such an affliction to befall you, you will be lost to this world!"

Amaz answered, "I understand." His heartbeat increased with fear, but I knew he did not comprehend.

Navarhys turned back to me.

"I was not alone," I spoke up to defend myself. "Tahlia was with me!"

"Tahlia is not an escort," Medina commented.

Navarhys looked at his stepmother and she looked away embarrassed at what had transpired.

Navarhys grew angrier as he turned and looked back at me. "I told you to stay in the home until I secured a guard for you."

I tried to grasp for reason, "The gardens are not part of your home?"

He tightened his grip on my arm, pulled me closer and looked fiercely into my eyes. He curled his lips but then just as quickly, he let go and turned away. "Go to your room. Stay there."

Later, Navarhys stormed into my quarters. He stood within inches of me, "Why do you disobey me?"

"I did not know that you meant for me to not leave the house."

"I told you not to!"

"You told me not to leave the home."

"You promised to do as I say."

"I thought I was doing that," I replied as tears brimmed my eyes. I was saddened because he was disappointed in me.

Seeing my tears, Navarhys looked away. As my tears fell, I looked up at him and saw a faraway look in his eyes. He thought of his free-spirited Aeyden.

Later in that week, Navarhys bought home Xio, my guard. He was a seventeen-year-old slave, trained to fight with his body and weapons since the age of five. He was solid wiry muscles. A darker brown than Tahlia and he was quiet. He had no facial hair. Tahlia told me that it was because he is a eunuch. I did not know what being a eunuch meant.

"How do you know all these things?"

"Growing up in a big city is different than country living. We learn and see many forbidden things."

"He is a eunuch. He is hairless where men should have hair. Forever a child."

"Why?" I asked Tahlia, throwing my dice against a wall. Xio stood above us, he heard it all.

"He does not have all his male parts."

Being a farm girl, I knew of male parts. "Which ones?"

She shrugged her shoulders. "I am not sure. I have never glimpsed a naked eunuch. Look at him. No hair on his face. He is as smooth as a baby."

I looked up at him and he quickly looked away. He bore not a sign of facial hair.

"Is what Tahlia tells me true?"

"Yes Mistress, I am as she says." He was ashamed of his difference.

I thought that to be sad. I could not fix him. "Come play with us."

"I am not to play with you. Only guard you."

"Is that what Navarhys told you?"

"Yes Mistress."

Navarhys would take me out on our horses sometimes. My horse's name was Sundown. His horse was named Majesty. I loved our time together. I am certain he enjoyed them too. We walked on the beach sometimes late in the day just before dinner. He would hold my hand, sometimes he would tell me tales, at other times he would listen to mine.

Now that I had Xio, I was permitted travel outside of our home and occasionally, outside of our gated quarter. I enjoyed going to the market and seeing the sights in the city. I had to inform Navarhys ahead of time. He kept tight restrictions on me. If I did anything he did not approve of, he would not let me leave the house for weeks. When I did venture out, I would do so two or three times in a week. Cutthroat Alley, a nickname for a rough area of the city, was strictly off-limits. The city outside the gated rich area was dirtier, smelled awful and some of its people ill-mannered and abusive; but I enjoyed the dealings and newness of it all. I think I enjoyed it because it was my second chance at childhood. I missed out once and I was determined to enjoy myself this time around.

Xio had to make sure that other men did not touch me. Navarhys detested that, above all things. Within the gated rich section, men saw my jewelry and the short dresses I wore and knew that I was spoken for. Outside the gates, the rules were not always observed. More than once, Xio had to threaten men that intentionally came too close or made inappropriate comments to me. I loved his dedication.

All three of us, Xio, Tahlia and I, walked three miles each way to the main market and back. I loved to walk. Xio did not complain, but Tahlia did. My poor companions. I felt their aches after our long day at the market and quietly eased them. The market outings gave me a chance to experience my new city. With my generous allowance, I bought interesting wares. Things that I had never seen or tasted before. I was not allowed to eat anything until Navarhys had a taster taste it. We occasionally went to the outskirts of the harbor. It was dangerous and I was not allowed to go too close. The beach was another of my favorite places. All types of people from our city and abroad went there to enjoy the sun and the warm waters that lapped at Nabu's shores.

Tahlia matured before I did. I congratulated her. She was not feeling well during her time. After it ended, Brahada cut Tahlia's beautiful long hair. We both cried together.

One day on our way to the market, we passed a house that had a gathering outside of it. Tahlia, on my instructions, inquired about what was going on.

"They say a highly regarded man, a chi, is dying in the home. He will leave behind seven children and a wife.

"Do you think I could see him?" I felt the sorrow of his family.

"No Mistress, this is not a place for you," Tahlia commented. "His is a belief of the very poor and that of some slaves."

Ignoring her concern, I turned to my guard, "Xio, see that I am granted access."

Xio placed his arm around mine, knowing he could not leave my side. Then demanded the crowd step aside for me. They did.

The old man lay on his bedding, deathly gray. His bare chest revealed ribs and attested to his shallow labored breathing.

"He has a sickness!" Xio stopped short. "You cannot continue towards him." I saw the determination in Xio eyes. He physically held me determined not to allow me to proceed any further.

I willed him to loosen his grip on me, and he did. "It is alright," I patted his arm. I enjoyed discovering my abilities.

I kneeled next to the dying man's wife. She prayed next to her husband's bedside. She looked towards me in despair.

"Is he a good husband to you?" I asked her gently patting her aged withered hand.

"Yes, he is." Tears streamed down her cheeks and I saw her memories of their shared love and life.

Though I knew, I asked anyway. "Is he a good father to his children?" She smiled with a nod her continued reminiscences. Her heart looked at him and saw his struggle to hang on.

"A kind soul deserves another chance." I placed my hand on his cold clammy chest. The heat from my hand sank into him. Color quickly returned to his skin and he began to breathe easier.

I stood. "I must go now."

The wife looked up at me. "Thank you. Even if he dies, thank you for your kind words."

His children and others thanked me also. I smiled graciously and proceeded to walk back the way I came.

A voice from behind me shouted, "It's a miracle!"

I turned back to see the man that lay close to death, struggling to rise. Two of his sons assisted him.

"Wait," his raspy voice spoke with practiced authority. "What is your name, young lady?"

"Star," I replied, not wanting my true name to be known.

"Star. You are a blessing." With help, he struggled to stand. One of his grown sons, came toward me, imploring me to return to him.

Xio yelled a warning in Katerian, pulling out his short blade. I stayed his hand.

"I apologize." He and his family bowed thanking me again and again. He turned searching beneath his bedding. "I give you this gold medallion." With help he offered it to me.

"Really, there is no need."

"I see that you are a maiden wife of a rich man." He read my wears. "Some young wives have a need to escape. With this medallion, you can buy your passage away from here."

"I will not leave my husband. He is good to me."

"Then you keep this." He held it out to me. Tahlia accepted it for me.

"You may need to help someone else one day.

"Thank you, Good Sir." I smiled and bowed my head towards him. As I left his residence, I pulled my image from all their minds to protect myself.

Navarhys did not return home that night or the following night. He and Andris were busy in his office for a good part of a week thereafter. I did not have to reveal my encounter. For that I was thankful. Navarhys may not understand my reasons.

I met Shadiya on one of our adventures in the main market one day as she shopped.

Greetings Shadiya." I called seeing her haggling with a vendor over the price of some fruits. Dressed in an immaculate cream-colored dress with a shimmery blue sash from her left shoulder down past her right hip down to her dress's hem near her ankles, she looked marvelous. Slaves did not dress that way. Her sandals were made of good leather, but she wore no jewelry and had no escort. She wore her flowing brown hair just below her shoulders.

She turned towards me a little surprised. "Greetings, Star Child. How goes things with you?"

I did not recall if Navarhys introduced us using my real name or the other. Rawnie probably told her that name, I thought to myself. I decided to let it pass. "Well, thank you, and with you?"

She smiled, "As well as could be expected."

"Your hair is growing. Why is that?"

"Master allows me to."

"Does he intend to free you?"

She shifted uncomfortably. "Maybe we should not be discussing the master's intent."

"I am freeborn, and I have asked you a question."

I saw that she did not want to answer, but she decided to. "Master has already freed me."

I had not known. Navarhys does not discuss her and guards his thoughts of her. "Then why do you still call him Master?"

"I have always called him Master. I will continue to do so."

"Why do you still stay?"

She looked at me crossly. "It is not easy to build a new life doing what I have done."

"So now you are just his whore?"

"Star Child, I do not want to discuss him. Master will hurt me." I felt fear rising in her.

I picked up a pear and pretended to examine it. I changed the subject. "Did you know Aeyden?"

"Star Child, I cannot discuss her, either."

"In future, if we meet, you will address me as Mistress, I am your master's wife."

"As you wish...Mistress." She looked at me wishing that she was where I was.

I looked at her wishing I could get the part of Navarhys that she commands.

"Mistress you should not be talking to her, Master would not like it," Tahlia offered as we walked away.

"He has not banned me from doing so."

Xio added, "I will have to tell the master that you met her."

Sweat formed on my body. "Why?" I looked towards him a little annoyed.

"The master has instructed me to tell him all."

I shrugged my shoulders. He would know anyway just by touching me. Unlike others, I could not hide many things from Navarhys, especially if the deed or thought was fresh in my mind. I hoped he would not be too angry.

That night we had guests. Navarhys met us as we approached the front door.

"Tahlia go prepare my wife's bath. Xio you are to stay by my wife's side until she retires." He kissed me on my cheek. I saw it in his eyes that he saw whom I had spoken to. "We will speak later. Right now, we have two special guests. They are both like me. I do not want you to touch either one of them. They are both extremely… promiscuous. His wife, Miarra is an imitator of form. She can become any living thing she touches or who touches her.

"Should I be rude?"

"No need. I have already informed them that you are a maiden and I would be offended should they approach you." He laced his arm in mine to escort me in and told me their names.

Lord Eli's good looks were not in a Nabian way, more like where I am from. He wore his blond wavy hair to his mid-back. Handsome Lord Eli had unique dazzling green eyes. Green eyes rolled over every inch of me. His wife's complexion was as white as any I have seen. Her hair, the opposite, the darkest of black and her lips almost unnaturally red. Lady Miarra, who stood slightly taller than I, had pale blue eyes that rolled over me in the same uncomfortable way her husband's eye had. Both left me with an exposed feeling.

"So how are you enjoying the city, Ahelia?" Lord Eli asked.

"I find something new in it every day, Lord Eli."

"She is allowed to go out?" Lady Miarra asked rather sharply.

"Yes," Navarhys answered. "I have her guarded at all times."

"Do you forget that she has gifts that have not been tamed? We cannot chance that she brings attention to us."

I did not like her. She was far too bossy and nosey.

I felt Navarhys's indecision. "She has not exhibited any tendency to use her gifts."

Lord Eli looked at me with a penetrating stare. I looked away kind of afraid, and sort of embarrassed. I did not like that he would look at me so. The thought of being kicked jumped into my head.

"Yes, she has."

I reddened. *'Could Eli read my thoughts?'*

"Yes, he can. You did not tell me about the mule."

"You knew I got kicked."

"You did not tell me that you got your revenge on it."

"I did not think I was responsible for what happened to the donkey."

Navarhys turned my face up to his and investigated, "Yes you did." Then he bought his lips to my ear, "Never lie to me."

"You Ahelia are capable of many things, especially when you are distressed." Lady Miarra stated sternly. "Be very careful when you are angry. You must not bring attention to us."

I looked to Navarhys and he nodded in agreement.

Not wanting him to be angry, I vowed, "I will be careful."

"Go," Navarhys indicated that I leave with Xio.

"A male guard? Are they related?" Eli inquired.

"No, he is a eunuch," Navarhys stated.

Lord Eli laughed deliciously.

Navarhys came to my bed that night.

He lay facing me. "I do not want you associating with Shadiya."

"Is it taboo that I speak with her?"

"If I say so, It is."

"Why?"

"You know why."

"Because she is your whore?"

"Wife, do not call her that!"

"You have feelings for her?"

"Do not associate with her!"

"Do you love her?"

"No, I do not love her."

"Does she know that?"

"Stop it! Stop asking about her." He changed turning a deep red. "It is none of your business!" His angry red eyes blazed back at me.

He made to leave but I flung my arms about him. "Please stay," I sobbed. "I will not mention her again, please!" I felt so good being near him.

He turned to me, kissing me full on the lips. His tongue played with mine. I felt his hands roaming my body, pulling me against him. I felt the hard ridge of his manhood pressed against me. His breathing quickened as did my heartbeat. Then he was gone. I opened my eyes. He stood beside my bed. His skin still a scarlet red but his sad eyes an iridescent yellow.

"I have to leave. We cannot…", he stormed from my room.

I smelled his whore on him the following morning. I was not pleased.

"Why do you get this way?" he asked at his wit's end. "You are aware of how things are…" *'between us.'*

"You could do as I do and wash her from your flesh before you greet me!"

"As you do?" his eyes darkened.

"I…I mean after I get back from the city, knowing I take with me the smells of many different people."

Navarhys did not speak to me during the rest of that morning. I do not see what his problem was, he knew everything about me.

"I do not want you to leave the house today," He requested.

"Your wish." I consented. It was his way of punishing me.

Amaz and his mother were away visiting.

Xio, Tahlia and I took this time to play hide and go seek. We played more freely when Navarhys, Amaz and Medina were not home. This home had many different interesting places to hide.

We still had to be watchful of Brahada. She was freeborn and a confidant of Navarhys. I have yet to see her object to one thing he says.

We took a break. During which we ate, and Tahlia taught Xio a few written words in English and Tarkarian. Xio learned quickly. She taught me the Tarkarian words also. Tahlia should not be a slave. Her freeborn father had her schooled in how to read, how to work with numbers and English, my language.

We resumed playing after lunch. Thankfully, Brahada was hard of hearing. She could not hear a sandstorm if it was upon her.

At one point in the game, Tahlia and I found ourselves hiding in the Library behind one of our bookshelves.

"You should not be here," I laughed hugging her. "We need to hide separately."

"I cannot go now Xio is nearby," she giggled trying to keep quiet.

We huddled down trying to stifle our bubbling laughter.

Tahlia looked up seeing Xio looking down on us. I turned, and we laughed more.

Xio smiled bending down to help us to our feet.

We walked from behind the bookshelf. Medina stood just inside the library's door.

"What were you three doing?"

I swallowed, thinking it could not look as bad as it seemed. "We were just playing a game."

"A game?" She looked at me angrily. She then turned to my distressed looking guard, "Xio, Navarhys will hurt you."

"This is not what you think," I pleaded.

"It is not important what I think."

"I will tell him," I stated afraid. "It would sound better and be more accurate coming from me."

She looked back at me, "I have to be there when you tell him."

"Why?"

"To be sure that you do, or I will have to."

I walked into Navarhys's arms just as he was about to meet with his assistant, Andris. Medina close at my heels.

He kissed me on my cheek. I held him, "Please do not be angry." He looked down at my tears and read me, and his fury exploded.

"Xio! What were you doing?"

"I was doing my duty, My Master."

Navarhys made to strike Xio.

"No Navarhys, he only did as I asked."

"You do not ask a slave anything. You issue orders!"

He looked from me to Xio then back to me. "Since he cannot do as I say, I will have to sell him."

"Please do not sell him." I tried to stifle a cry. "Please Navarhys. I am sorry." I held his left hand between mine.

"How could you beg for him? He is property!"

"Please do not sell him. It was my fault. Punish me."

He smiled, "I am punishing you."

'You punish me for not being Aeyden'

He heard my thoughts but made no reply.

"Please do not do this."

The next day Xio, my trusted guard was no more. Tahlia told me that his room was left bare as if no-one ever slept there. I was once again confined to the house.

I ate breakfast with Navarhys in silence. He did not try to engage me in conversation, and I kept my mind blank.

Tahlia taught me more words and the written Tarkarian in my bedroom. No-one would walk in on us there.

"I do not want you to hug me if we are not in my room," I told her. "I do not want him to know how much I care for you."

"Mistress I know." She cried with me. "We can only hope Xio is sold to a good master."

I could not sleep that night, so I secreted myself to our roof. Navarhys and Andris sometimes entertained there. I went to the bench on the far side, lay down and looked up towards the stars. Spotting the brightest star, I thought of Tomas. On clear nights did he look at these stars and think of me? Did he speak to them as I do? Was he looking at the same bright star as I was at this very moment? I think I missed him at that very moment more than I had since moving here to live with Navarhys.

"I am sure he misses you too."

I did not look towards him. "How did you know I was here?"

"I hear your thoughts."

I disliked him reading my private thoughts.

"We share a single soul Wife. I cannot help but read you."

He came to lay down next to me. "I do not like that you are sad. You make friends with these slaves. You should not. They are property."

"You lay with your slave. Is she not more than just a slave?"

"She is no longer my slave." He placed his fingers on my chin moving my face towards his, both his face and eyes darkening. "But surely, you knew that."

He quickly regained his human form, "I do not wish to fight with you. Xio had to go." He kissed me on the lips, then he shifted so that I lay in his arms. His presence infused feelings of harmony and peace into me.

"Has anyone ever told you that you shine just from the starlight?"

"No, Navarhys, no one has."

"Well, you do." He kissed me on my lips.

We fell asleep together for the first time since I move here to live with him.

I woke feeling every cell in my being, tingling with happiness. Navarhys's closeness made me feel so wonderful.

Two days before my sixteenth birthday I began to bleed. I did not feel the joy that I thought I would. I cried.

"Tahlia, please do not tell him." I pleaded to try to hide the evidence.

"If I dare not tell Master, you will be left with no slaves."

He came to my room soon afterward. "You are still trying to hide things from me." He regarded me angrily, his eyes a deep red.

I now had a new status and with this new status, I now wore long dresses down to my ankle. He had a dressmaker come in to measure me. He bought me a whole new wardrobe of fabulously designed dresses. Navarhys had Brahada donate all my childhood dresses to the poor

He replaced my bracelets with a simple gold ring.

Amaz was horrified. He grumbled that I would soon have a whelp to further deny his right to inherit his stepfather's estate.

"Amaz you should go find your happiness somewhere other than here. You obviously, are not happy here." I tire of his braying. He did not know Navarhys fully, but I knew his mother did.

"I should at least be granted fifty percent of everything."

"You do not have your stepfather's name. Why should you be given half?"

"He had a hand in raising me."

"You are not suffering."

"Amaz! Stop bothering Star. She has nothing to do with you quarrel with Navarhys."

"She will carry his child."

"Stop Amaz. Stop pestering her."

"You, mother, should be defending me. I only seek what is best for both of us."

"Navarhys has seen to our needs. Amaz! Stop it!"

I felt myself getting angry with Amaz and his ungratefulness.

Navarhys did not come to me the night he could or for many many nights after that. I felt his neglect deeply. I thought he waited like he had said, for me to mature. Now I had matured, but he still did not come. I wondered if Aeyden still came between us. It saddened me to go over our situation in my mind. He began to avoid me. I hardly saw him during our meals and when I saw him during the day, he was always rushing around with Andris.

The household and the slaves knew I was still a maiden. I would walk in on them discussing me or comparing me to Aeyden.

My embarrassment and sadness, almost too much for me to bear.

One day I heard a commotion coming from our courtyard. I went to see what it was all about. As I reached the bottom of the stairs, I stopped in absolute shock. There in our inner hall stood Tomas. I burst out in tears. We ran to one another, hugging each other tightly. "I have missed you!" I missed Tomas the most out of anyone else in this world, even my own mother.

"Here too Little Sis." I felt his breath on my neck.

"I did not know you were coming." Tahlia handed me a napkin and I smiled up at him.

"Navarhys wanted to surprise you."

I looked around. There he stood looking at us with his brilliant orange yellowy eyes. I smiled at him very happy. I went to him and thanked him for this surprise.

"You are going to dislike me," he joked. "…because I need Tomas with me for the next few days."

"Really?" I worded worriedly.

"Then he is yours." He smiled my way.

I nodded happily.

Tomas, his two men, Navarhys and a few of his men left, while the belongings of Tomas and his two men were bought in.

I retired to my room in the midst of it all. Navarhys would not like that I continue in the presence of the male slaves.

As I settled for an afternoon nap, Tahlia burst into my room, tears streaming down her face. "Come, Mistress. Come quickly."

"What is it?"

She dragged me out of the room. "Xio is in the stables and he is badly hurt!"

My stomach heaved with fear and dread and my mind raced. *How was he hurt? What is he doing here? This will lead to trouble*, I sensed it already. Xio lay among the hay curled up beneath a horse blanket, blood everywhere about him.

The three slaves that stood around him discussed where they would bury him. They parted as Tahlia and I entered.

"What happened to him?" I screamed. I had not been expecting the distressing sight that I saw along with the coppery smell of blood that tasted in the back of my throat.

The slave Akim spoke, "His master beat him, Mistress."

"That bad? What did he do?" I cried.

"He ran, but they caught him."

I cried stooping down then pulling the blanket off him. I saw that he did not want me to see him.

"Tau get him some clothes from my brother's room. Tahlia go to my room, bring all of my allowance and the gold medallion."

"Mistress, I cannot steal your brother's clothes. Master will sell me." Tau protested sounding rightfully distressed. All of Navarhys's slaves feared him, but they were not treated badly if they abided his rules. He did not tolerate stealing, lying and or disobeying.

"I have given you an order." I looked at him vexed. "Now go!"

I read his thoughts. *'Listening to you is how Xio got himself into this mess.'*

"I will inform my brother when he returns. You will not have to worry about Navarhys."

I turned back to Xio. He wore a dirty piece of bloody cloth about his waist. Blood seeped out of some of the long welts on his body.

"Xio do not be ashamed." I leaned closer to him. "Put your arms around me. I will heal you."

"Mistress, I cannot, he will…"

"Shss…" I place my arms around him. His feverish body shook and trembled from pain. I sense as his body rejuvenated and healed in my arms.

Tau returned with some of Tomas's clothes. I felt confident that Xio would not look like a slave in them even with his shaved head. He could pass as a traveler.

"Quickly Xio, help him off with those rags. Xio stood unsteadily. The wounds were gone but the blood from his beating remained on his flesh.

"Tau get a bucket with water quickly. Tahlia go get food from the kitchen and do not let Brahada or Medina see you!"

"Yes, Mistress."

The slaves helped him wash. He dressed, and I pressed the gold medallion into his palm first. "This… to buy your passage onto a ship." Then I gave him the satchel with my allowance. I was not using it anyway because I no longer went to the market. "This… to help you start a new life."

Xio looked at me adoringly. "You are a blessing just like the Chi said. I will forever be grateful to have known you. I cannot …" he cried, though he tried not to. "I cannot express how very thankful I am." He reached out for my hand then and kissed me there. I felt his tears of gratitude run over the back of my hand and I smiled.

I hugged him knowing his fear would not let him reciprocate. "Climb the back wall, stay out of sight until you get to the docks. Buy your way out of here."

That night Navarhys, Andris, Tomas, and their contingent did not return. They were away for close to a week. Upon their return, I made sure Navarhys, Andris and Tomas each had a hot bath ready for them.

I went to Tomas's room while Zek, a slave, assisted him to bathe. The slave looked at me as if I was doing something forbidden. I chose to ignore him.

"How was your journey brother?"

"Navarhys is a great man. I am happy that he is your husband…"

"…But?"

"I hear that he does not welcome you to his bed."

"Who told you that?" I spat very upset that he knew.

"I hear the slaves talking about you."

"They speak in English?"

"I have learned a considerable amount of Tarkarian from my men and the slaves that Navarhys gave to me."

Tears brimmed my lids. "Navarhys is good to me. He is sensitive to my needs."

Tommie rose out of the bath, took a towel from Zek and wrapped it around his waist. He came to me and looked at me the way he did when I was hurting as a crippled child. He was the first person to touch my soul. "He is not sensitive to all your needs." He knew me too well.

"Shss……he will know what you've said to me." I placed my thumb on his lips.

"I want him to know." He smiled slowly, wiping away a tear from my cheek with his thumb. "I want you to be completely happy." He kissed the cheek that he had just wiped.

The door burst open and there stood Navarhys looking at my brother and me. To him, we looked intimate. Navarhys changed to a deep crimson and he grew in height. Zek went to his knees.

"What are you doing here?" His voice roared in my ears.

Tommie jumped away from me, holding onto his towel. "We were only…" Tommie tried to intercede on my behalf.

"I am not speaking to you, Brother." Navarhys's voice reverberated about the room. He narrowed his eyes at Tommie. He then looked again towards me.

"I just wanted a word with my brother. I do not get much time with him."

"Brother is in his bedchamber nude and you felt that you just had to speak to him now?"

I looked towards frightened Tommie, then back towards my husband. "We are siblings. We have seen one another naked on many occasions. We do not think anything of it."

He bridged the distance between us instantly. He grabbed my arm, pulling me against himself. "You disappoint me. This is not behavior appropriate for my wife."

"Navarhys, I…"

He growled, "Confine yourself to your room!"

I began to tear. "He's my brother. We were talking. You know that is all that we were doing! Why do you…"

"Do…as…I…say!"

I sobbed running from that room, up the stairs, into my room. I slammed the door and flung myself on top of my bed. I felt anger towards him. He knew we were not doing anything, and I hated his ugly implication.

Not too long afterward Navarhys came to my room with the three male slaves. He ordered them to take my trunk with my clothes out of my room and into his. They were ordered to strip my bedroom, including the curtains and after they left, he ordered me to strip. I tearfully complied. He left me with only a single bedsheet, nothing else. He locked my door that led out to the hallway.

His intent evident; to be my only contact. He bought my meals and took my bedpan when needed. I wondered if Tommie was still here in Nabu, or if Navarhys had sent him away. The prospect sickened my heart. I could not bear to think on it. I also worried if Tahlia was still here. Maybe he had sold her. Navarhys did not like me to be too close to him or anyone. Would I ever dislike someone so much that I would keep them away from everyone they loved? I do not think so.

Luckily Nabu was a hot place and I did not suffer from the cold. Navarhys did not speak to me for the first two days though I begged him to reconsider what he was doing to me. He attended me in silence. I stopped trying to convince him and became more silent myself. I tried not to show on my face how very upset I was. He knew though, he could feel it. My heart ached so very much with injustice. I tried not to eat on the fourth day of my confinement, but he put a stop to that.

"Eat, Wife!" he ordered reddening.

I looked at him scornfully.

With one touch he left me ravenous and very thirsty. I could not help myself. I could not go on without nourishment. I hated him for that.

I would not look his way on day five, whilst he watched me eat breakfast. I turned my back to him when he came to my room to deliver my lunch. He put a stop to that also.

"If you continue to ignore me, I will send Brother away. You will never see him again."

I turned towards him, glad to know that Tommie was still here in Nabu, but I could not prevent the overflow of tears inside me. "I have not done anything wrong!"

"You have."

"Yes, I was born Ahelia and not Aeyden."

He turned crimson; his eyes glowed like red embers. I felt his fury and the heat emitted of his body. He stormed over to me. Through clenched teeth, he spat, "You try to blame everything on her, but you will not this time. You will apologize to me for your wayward behavior."

"I am sorry I am not Aeyden."

He lashed out at me and slapped me hard across my face. I fell, crumpled to the ground bawling my eyes out. "I hate you!" I felt his heartbreak. I felt it as if it was my own or maybe it was? "I hate being here!" I felt regret. I sobbed blocking our souls' mirroring feelings from my heart. It made me feel so very alone. I had forgotten how that felt. Feeling only myself within my body. I saw in his eyes that he felt the same way. I covered my face in my arms. I wanted to be away from him. "Send me back home to my mother." When I finally looked up, he was gone. I cried more that night than I had ever in my life. Not even when I was injured by the donkey, did I cry as much as I did then. I hated this place. I hated being his wife. I wished I was somewhere else, anywhere else. I no longer felt that I could find happiness here. He read all my thoughts and I was glad that he could.

He stealthily bought my breakfast to me the next day. I looked up and there he stood. Our eyes met briefly. I felt our distance in that one glance. Our hearts were saddened. He made his presence known when he bought my lunch for me, but he remained silent. He sat looking at me as I ate. I saw the hurt in his eyes. Both times after I had finished eating, he kissed me on the corner of my lips. The moment he touched me, I felt at peace with him. Afterward, he left me feeling lonesome.

Tahlia came with two of the other slaves that afternoon. "Mistress, the master wants you fresh for dinner." The two slaves carried water for the bath.

"I do not want to!"

"Mistress, please do as Master says," she tried coxing me. She cried looking at the bruise on my cheek, at the bare room and then at me, wrapped in the solitary soiled sheet. The master has purchased a brand-new dress for you. Look at it." Tahlia presented the long satin purple dress with a cream-colored sash. "Is it not beautiful Mistress?"

Still filled with anger, I did not answer her. The other slaves left the room.

"Come, Mistress." She felt the temperature of the water. "It is how you like it, hot."

"I do not want to dine with him."

"Please!" She pleaded. "Please do as Master asks." I looked at her and sensed her distress. "Master will separate us. Please come. I will help you bathe. Please!"

We cried and I complied. I did not have a choice. He knew how to trap me into doing his bidding.

As I stepped out of the bath, Navarhys came. Tahlia wrapped a towel around me.

"Leave us!" Navarhys put out to Tahlia. She bowed her head and left us.

He gestured towards the bed. I sat, and he sat down next to me.

"It was unbecoming of me to hit you. I hope that you will forgive me." He rubbed the back of his fingers over my swollen cheek, taking away the bruising and tenderness.

I shied away from his touch. He reached over to hold me around my waist pulling me against his body. He felt warm and soothing.

He kissed me on my cheek. "Do you like your new dress, Wife?"

I nodded and my tears fell.

"I need to hear you." He voiced barely above a whisper; I felt his breath tickle my ear.

"It is lovely, Navarhys." I still did not look his way.

"I want to see you wear it." He stated gently.

"I am still wet."

"Come, I will dry you." He tugged at my hand slightly and I complied. I stood as he rubbed me dry, eying my body. "You have changed." He looked at me with his orange-yellowy eyes and I felt like I was at sea once again drifting. I donned the dress. It fit me very well.

"You look lovely."

"Thank you," I replied not believing him.

He stood to embrace me, and I felt his arousal. He looked into my eyes and my heartbeat quickened. He smiled knowing that I responded to him. "I have unlocked your door."

I nodded turning to look away from him. He thought of my brother seeing me the way he had just seen me. "Be sure you and Brother are never alone together." He turned my face back to him, his strange eyes touching me somewhere deep.

 "As you wish Husband."

He kissed me full on my lips while looking deeply into my eyes. My heart pounded against him. He smiled knowing the effect he had on me.

"Rawnie is here. She wants to meet with you."

My heart was happy, but I did not show it on my face. Rawnie was one of the few people that Navarhys allowed to come by as she wished.

He walked me out to the parlor on the first floor. Rawnie sat sipping wine talking with Tahlia and Brahada. "I will come for you when dinner is ready."

I nodded and he kissed me on my cheek.

Rawnie saw the hurt on my face. She came to me and hugged me without words. Once again, I found myself in tears.

"He hates me." I confided in her.

"Shsss…He does not. The words your heart believes will become your universe."

"You do not know what he has done to me."

"I know." She rubbed my back in sympathy. "Star Child use your voice. It is your first strength." She turned and ushered me towards the back door. "Come let us sit together on this beautiful afternoon." We went out to the veranda. I knew how a prisoner feels after feeling freedom and sunlight on their face for the first time after confinement. It feels like heaven visited upon the earth.   However, your heartbeat was before, after freedom it beats with such joy; you feel you could explode. "Rawnie and I sipped on wine waiting for dinner to be ready. Tahlia sat close by. Brahada excused herself to supervise the dining arrangements.

"I know you are still a virgin." Rawnie smiled over at me.

I looked at Tahlia. She looked away.

"Someone should not be telling tales." Why I thought, am I such a topic for everyone? Surely there is something more interesting in this house to be talked about.

"She did not tell me. I know."

I looked at Rawnie and sensed that she was telling the truth. "Was he a good lover to your daughter?"

"She did not complain."

I stifled a cry.   "Why does he not love me?" I still clung to hope. I wished for it dearly. I wanted to be the one he loved, mainly because I knew that I loved him.

"He does love you. He fights it." She looked me in the eyes. "And he will love you the way that you wish."

I smiled a sad smile because I still did not believe.

She sipped a little wine. "With each passing day, you grow dearer in his heart."

"No, he does not like me." I just could not allow myself to believe that he did and get disappointed. "But if we become intimate, maybe then he will like me just a little bit."

"You sell yourself cheaply Star. This intimacy you so crave may happen much more sooner than you think." She smiled raising her glass and took a sip.

I changed the subject. "Is my brother here?"

She nodded with a smile, "Come."

Tommie sat watching his men practicing swordplay. When he saw me, I saw the relief in his eyes. He started coming toward me. I ran into his arms.

"Are you alright, Little Sis?"

I nodded. "I thought he had dismissed you and I would not get to see you again," I cried.

He held me tighter then placed me at arm's length, looking at me in my new dress, "You look beautiful."

"No, I am not. I am ugly."

"Why would you say such a thing? You have always been beautiful." He looked annoyed with me.

"You say that because you are my brother, but I know that I am ugly."

"Is that what he tells you?" Tommie hugged me once again and I hugged him.

"He does not have to tell me."

I felt his heartbeat quicken. He released me and stepped away. I turned and there Navarhys stood by the back door.

"Come Wife." He held out his hand to me and I went to him. He read me of course. "You are not ugly," he whispered in my ear. "I do not mean for you to feel that way."

Chapter Four

Navarhys sat at the head of our table, I sat to his left, Tommie sat opposite me, to his right side. Tommie's two men sat beside him. Rawnie sat next to me. Andris sat at the other end of the table facing Navarhys. As we sat to eat at our table for a simple dinner of lamb, rice, fruit, and wine. We got an unexpected visitor. It was a tall gentleman, wearing purple-dyed silks. He demanded the return of the slave we named Xio.

"Why would we have him?" Navarhys asked perplexed. I willed myself not to show how nervous I had become.

"I heard it told…" He came into our eating hall trailing Navarhys, "… that your child bride and he were …associated."

Navarhys turned on him. "Repeat that and I will ruin you!"

"I meant no disrespect. Only that you bought him for her, and he was always in her presence. I could not have meant anything else; he is a eunuch."

Navarhys composed himself, turned to me and asked. "Do you know the whereabouts of Xio,
Wife?"

I looked into his sand-colored eyes and answered truthfully, "No, I do not." He held my gaze a moment longer and saw the stories of both the Chi and Xio's that I held hidden from him.

He turned to our visitor, "Mr. Nypliato will that be all?"

They exchanged light pleasantries, then Navarhys asked Andris to see him to the door.

I trembled to know that he had seen.

"Why Wife?" He asked after we heard the front door slam closed.

"Why what?" I replied defiantly.

"He is someone else's property."

"If I had not saved him, he would still be missing a slave today."

"He is property!" He slammed his hand on the table causing me to jump.

I felt my temper rise. "So am I!" I retorted.

He looked at me, stunned. "You are my wife."

"I sat at my dining table and saw as my father sold me to you!"

"Wife, you know better.   You are not property." He was really upset at what I said, more so than it appeared to our guests.

I see now that he regretted saying anything to me here, but I persisted. "Yes, I am. I just shine better."

I saw his tears fill his lower eyelids. "Wife you are not property."

"You treat me like property," I added bitterly. "I did not take your Aeyden's life. Is that not right Rawnie?"

Rawnie who had sat silently with our other guests answered, "Star is correct, Navarhys."

Andris stepped back into our dining hall.

Navarhys reached over to me and kissed me on my lips. He then whispered in my ear, "You know you are not to show your gifts."

I whispered back, "I pulled the memory of those that saw."

A conversation at the table started up slowly again, but I noticed that Andris stared intently at me from his end of the table. My discomfort at Andris's continued scrutiny became obvious even to Navarhys.

"Andris! Navarhys growled, "Your impertinent regard of my wife is extremely offensive." Navarhys's voice sounded unearthly. His skin darkened to his fallen crimson and his eyes darken to their reddish-brown.

The room, once again, fell silent.

"I...I... had not realized that I was staring. I must have...."

"Let it be the last time!" Navarhys growled menacingly baring his fangs.

Andris bowed his head yielding to Navarhys.

Thank you I directed at Navarhys.

Navarhys looked towards me and for a moment his eyes softened, returning to their usual hue and the crimson faded from his skin. His eyes, however, returned to their angered reddish-brown for the remainder of our meal. If I had not known better, I would have accused him of jealousy. I began to unblock the wall I had erected to shield my fragile heart.

Navarhys, Andris, Tomas and the men went out to a man's gathering out in the desert. I did not know what that meant and did not inquire because I was not sure I wanted to know.

Upon my return to my bedroom, all my belonging had been replaced and once again my bedroom felt familiar and welcoming.

Rawnie insisted Tahlia draw another scented bath. I watched Rawnie put in something extra as I soaked.

"What is that?" I asked not too concerned.

"It will make him more amorous, less shy." She smiled wickedly. "A gypsy potion."

I mirrored her smile.

He came into my room late that night, naked. His skin shimmered gold-like from candlelight. This is how I saw him the very first time I had seen him in my dreams. He lay down next to me pulling me on top. Kissing me he rolled on top of me. Still, our lips wrestled. His body blanketed mine in his warmth. The feel of his silky feeling sex rubbing my upper thigh, did things to my stomach. His wet warm tongue slid inside me searching out my tongue. They played together as he reached for my hands and held them just beside my shoulders. Navarhys thrust himself into me. I bit his tongue through the pain. I tried to pull away, but he pulled out slightly then pressed his body into me deeper. He stifled my cry with his chest. Again, he surged into my body seeming to rip me in half.

"I can't! I cannot do this."

He guided my head, so we kissed. I tasted his blood on his tongue.   I tried to push his tongue out using mine, but he persisted. Pushing deep into me. Navarhys did not stop. He still joined with me forcefully, bringing me to the brink of my endurance.

Just as I opened my mouth to scream, he stopped and held me tightly. *"I am sorry."* Feelings of calm tranquility descended upon us both. We both felt afloat. So forceful were these feelings of harmony, I no longer felt my discomfort. *"*I should not be so...with you." His tears fell onto me. Stroking my hair, Navarhys kissed me slowly and I cried as well. "Where are my manners?" He continued to kiss me gently. He kneaded my breasts, kissing them and sucking them too. He moved inside me slowly.

"Move against me, Star," he whispered.

'I do not know how.'

He reached down with both his hands to my hips and showed me how. The discomfort returned. He bit my ear, I jerked away. He trailed kissed down my throat to my breasts sucking and licking at me, all the while he moved within me.

The assault on my senses slowly began to work. I began to respond to him, moving my hips slowly at first. He groaned. I began to welcome his body into mine. His tongue and teeth on my breast made his joining feel like a sweet massage. My nipples hardened and my body tightened around him, eliciting another groan from him. Navarhys thrust himself into me kissing me and nipping between my mouth and on my body. He demanded his due and I took pleasures from him this time. My heartbeat quickened but fear is what I felt.

"Trust me," he uttered in that voice of his that reverberated about us.

My body shuddered around him first, then the crests of uncontrollable emotional release shot through me. I cried out lost in ecstasy. I moved against him frantically hoping to build on power overtaking me. Navarhys took me rougher feeling my need. He began with a low guttural growl which reverberated both our bodies. His body heated and changed shedding his human form. He grew and my body reacted with a momentary inner pain changing quickly to a sexual quiver. His growl increased in intensity, as he did his grip. I cried out lost to need, desire, want. His essence spilling deep within me.

We lay in each other's arms for a long time afterward without speaking. Our deep breaths filled the air. His body radiated soothing heat. I felt so very happy being with him this way. I did not want him to let me go. My head rested on his chest. I heard felt his heartbeat pounding through his body and mine in rhythm with his.

"I have never felt anything like that before in my life."

Smiling he rolled on top of me. Navarhys kissed my earlobe, the one he bit and with his thumb and forefinger he healed the tenderness. He first licked at then kissed the remaining tears on my cheek. "I want to apologize for all that I have done to you. I hate that, because of me the slaves talk about you. I know that you and your brother, are just siblings and nothing more. You are so marvelous. I should have performed my husbandry duties long ago."

Feeling at peace knowing he felt the same way, I replied, "Yes you should have."

" I am gifting Tahlia to you."

"You are giving her to me?" I asked very surprised that he would let go control of Tahlia.

"Yes." He lay beside me once again.

I smiled and kissed his cheek. "Will I be getting a gift every night?"

He looked at me smiling, "You are presumptuous."

"I am optimistic, or will I have to wait another lifetime for an encore?"

He smiled a sad smile. His thoughts were of Aeyden.

He looked at me and knew that I read him.

"Forgive me. I miss her." He hugged me again.

"I know," I answered also feeling his sadness.

"I want you to know that I do not hate you." He hugged me, "Give me time."

"We have a lifetime Navarhys."

Chapter Five

Tomas and I spent three lovely days together. He took me to the city. I walked around my old haunts. He took me to a musical play given at an oasis in the desert. I had my first city tour by carriage, and he allowed me to steer but he had to assist me. It was not proper for me, a lady, to steer a carriage around in the city. I enjoyed walking inside our gated quarter. We had a park, a play area for children, benches and a small man-made pond and a small trail designed for walking.

I thoroughly enjoyed Tomas's company. He told me he built another home on his land. This one made from stone. Navarhys had ordered him to demolish the old wooden home. Too many people witness what had happened on the night of my birth. The twins worked on the farm whenever they came home. Paul is in training as a squire at Lord Chester's castle. Tony apprentices as a blacksmith in the village. Brian usually drunk, did little. Mama missed me terribly. Papa bought land elsewhere but sold it and decided to combine his resources with Tomas. They have tripled the size of the farm since I last saw it. They employ many village people during the harvest.

"Do Mom and Dad look the same?" I asked thinking of them both.

"I think they both show their age."

I felt sad. I can see why it was better to not move too far away from your family. A constant ache resides just below your heart for home. To me, that place was a safe place where every little move I made is not scrutinized. I was freer in movement, in what I could do and in what I could say and speak to.

Later that night after a marvelous session of lovemaking with Navarhys, he looked into my eyes and asked, "Are aware that your brother is in love with you?"

I laughed. Navarhys thought anything male was a danger to me somehow.

"No really." His eyes darkened. "He will not act on it though; I have turned him."

"No, he would not act on it because that is wrong." I laughed again. "He admires me Navarhys. He has told me that since I was a little girl." I looked at Navarhys strangely. "What do you mean by 'turned him'?"

"I mean I have infected his body with fluids from my own and because of that he cannot act against me."

"That is what you did this at Reine's home in my fourteenth year?"

"Yes."

"I felt the difference within him." I recalled the time in Reine's home and how unsure I was on how to react to what he was doing. "Medina, Brahada, Rawnie…"

"Not Rawnie, she already knew me. I do not turn those who willingly follow me."

"What about me?"

"You and I could not help ourselves." He smiled kissing me. "We could not help ourselves." He repeated looking at me with what I hoped was love.

On Tahlia's eighteenth birthday I granted her freedom.

"Do you know what this means?"

"You are no longer a slave." I stated with a smile, then added quieter, "You may leave me."

"No, I must marry. My father planned all along to free me after I matured. He planned to have me married. That is why I had private tutors. But then he died, and his spiteful wife sold my mother and me. My father is dead so Navarhys will be the one to find me a husband."

"If you were still a slave, he would not honor your father's wishes, why would he now?"

"It is a matter of honor. I am not property now."

"I do not believe you." If that be the case, I was not r freeing her. She would be leaving one cage just to be delivered to another. I rushed out towards the library, knocked and entered before I was asked to.

Navarhys, Andris, Tomas, and three strangers, two of them men, sat around talking and drinking tea. Zek, one of the slaves, dressed in proper clothes, attended them.

"Is it true Navarhys, once Tahlia is freed you will find her a husband?"

He looked at me crossly, his eyes glowed orange. I knew that I was not to interrupt his meetings.   "We will discuss Tahlia at a later time. Confine yourself!"

"She is the vision in the painting!" The eldest gentleman stated with an awed looked on his face.

I knew just then that these guests were all fallen.

The woman among them shook her head in agreement, "Yes."

I felt Navarhys's deep anger towards me.

A bustling at our front gate could be heard from where we were in the library. We all turned towards the sounds. Navarhys order me, once again to my room. Tomas's men took up arms. Navarhys did not have any of his paid henchmen at home at that time.

From my viewpoint in my bedroom, I saw as one of the slaves ran towards the house. A very fancy carriage got granted access beyond our wall. The unannounced guests were ushered into our tearoom. I heard a low rumble of male voices.

Andris came to my room, followed by a well-dressed stranger. My blood ran cold seeing Amaz trailing this unfamiliar person.

"There she is, the Star Child." Amaz pointed me out.

"Hello, Good Sir. I do not believe we have been properly introduced. Please forgive my brother-in-law, he is sometimes a little brutish." I made eye contact with Amaz. He smiled evilly back at me.

The gentleman bowed his head graciously. "I am Prince Adir of Nabu. Please to make your acquaintance, Madam."

"I am Ahelia, wife to Navarhys Xander, the pleasure is all mine, Your Highness." I bowed.

"I am keeping Navarhys below so that I can have a word with you separately.

I connected with Navarhys mentally and knew the story to tell.

"Anything this madman has told you is false," I stated not taking my eyes of Amaz.

"I am as sane as she is. She is the Star Child."

"I am no child, there is his first lie." I looked at him angrily. Are there no ends what he would do to get what he does not deserve? "This man is angry that I have repeatedly denied his advances under this very roof his brother has provided for him, no less."

"Madam, I am instructed by my father, the king of Nabu, to present you to him."

"I am not this Star Child that you seek."

"Amaz here has made mention of you." The prince sat on a chair and indicated that I sit also. I did along with Tahlia, on my bed. "Interestingly, another from a foreign country sings the same tale and has made mention of a Star Child also. Maybe Amaz is wrong and the foreigner will not know you. As it stands now, we are being accused by the crown of Lichenia of stealing a national treasure."

"He wants control of my husband's businesses. That is why he tells these lies." My tears filled my eyes.   "I was raised humbly on a farm. My husband was passing by one day, saw me and fell hopelessly in love with me. That is why I am here."

"I am sorry Madam; I have to escort you to the palace. Our foreigner is here with an escort from the King of Lichenia."

"I may be with child; I do not know if I could suffer such a journey."

"It is said, that you are still a virgin." The prince smiled smugly. "Your marriage could easily be annulled by my father." He stated as if he thought I would be pleased.

"You hear incorrectly. I have been with my husband many times."

"Your claims sound genuine." He smiled again, "But so do the men I have spoken too."

Navarhys read my thoughts as I had his, our stories were seamless.

I witness another 'turning' on this trip. The carriage rolled along, as we sat silently inside the prince's carriage. Navarhys sat beside me holding my hand and speaking to me gently and communicating in our way. *'He is observing us.'* I read Navarhys's thoughts. Tahlia sat next to the prince. I had insisted on my handmaiden coming with us. Normally a prince would not sit next to a servant, so I knew what my husband thought was true; he did so to observe us.

Without warning, Navarhys changed. The prince tried to cry out, but my husband moved fast clamping his hand over his mouth. Navarhys bit into his finger with his sharpen fang then stuck his now elongated sharpened nail into the prince's chest, just below his ribs.

The prince's eyes rolled backward. Navarhys retracted his nail, melted back to his human form and resumed sitting in the seat beside me. He held my hand replenishing his energy.

I looked at Tahlia, who sat beside the prince. She had not flinched during the entire event. It finally occurred to me that she had been turned too. When had that happened? I had not sensed it. Navarhys did not usually turn slaves.

'She is no longer a slave and may one day leave us.' I read his thoughts and understood them.

"Prince Adir, who is the foreigner that awaits us?"

The prince looked at me. "The one who says he is a brother to the star child."

"Is he deformed in any way?"

"Yes, he bears the form of a hand on his left cheek and a hand that is deformed and crippled."

Navarhys looked at me knowingly. *'I will take care of him.'*

I did not know it then, but at that very moment, Brian became deaf, blind and mute. He died on the streets of this foreign land in a matter of weeks.

"What of the royals in my wife's homeland?"

"The stories of the Star have long been circulated as well as that of the farmhouse it stood over. I journeyed there to see all for myself. I found a small keep, not a wooden farmhouse. I found a thriving farm, dairy, and stables with fine horses. I also found Brian, the disfigured village drunk. I listened to his ranting and learned a few things."

"Continue!"

"He told me who he was and about the old farmhouse. He told me of the foreigner that came and took his sister away left him and a fellow villager crippled. He introduced me to Daniel. Both remembered the tortured ass and what is widely believed about that ass by the villagers."

"How did you find us?"

"Your marriage is registered with the local church of the town and the crown had news of your journey there thanks to a spy named Sir Cooke who trailed you when you were there."

"Why did the crown not stop us from leaving?"

"The crown had lost interest in the star child after her injury. At the time of your departure, they had not realized that your bride was that child because your bride was not crippled."

"You will deliver us back to my home and you will tell the King that Amaz tripped, bumped his head then, could only mumble nonsense. Tell them that you visited my home and saw my wife, a woman too old to be the star child that was spoken of. Is that understood?"

"Yes, I understand."

We were delivered back to our front gates. Amaz emerged from one of the carriages, a bumbling buffoon. Navarhys refuse to have him enter our home. He housed him with his mother elsewhere until he could arrange something more advantageous.

Lord Eli and Lady Miarra returned to our home. They with Navarhys and Andris discussed at length, the situation with the royals. I had seen Andris's eye change in the past, but I knew for sure now, that he was also a fallen. I did not understand why I have a problem reading him.

"…They will be back. We have two choices. You and Star can leave, go into hiding or…" Navarhys, not happy to be a part of this plan, I watched Lady Miarra take my hand and duplicate my features. She looked and sounded just like me. Then she aged herself on purpose. I thought she was amazing. I did not have that gift.

Eli was to take me to his island for safekeeping. This worried my husband. "You cannot touch my wife Eli."

"You have mine." Lord Eli smiled handsomely.

"I will not be inappropriate towards Miarra."

"If you ask her…" Lord Eli shrugged his shoulders. Lady Miarra smiled expectantly.

"Eli, I would like that our friendship continues. Any advances on my wife would be seen by me as a breach of trust. I would prefer to leave with her and go into hiding than to think you may…"

Lord Eli held up his hand, "I would not Navarhys. I was only jesting. She is your chosen, I would guard her as if she mine."

It was agreed that Tomas's stay to be extended to confirm that Miarra, in my form, was his sister. Tahlia would come with me.

In his bed that night Navarhys mirrored my sadness.

"Do you find Lady Miarra attractive?" I asked.

He laughed.

"I do not see what is funny. She would sleep with you and Lord Eli would not care."

He kissed me, "Forbid me and I will not."

"I forbid you to sleep with her."

He smiled. "I wish I could do the same with you."

"What do you mean?"

"I will leave you with Eli and if anything happens to me, you... will be his."

"You would give me to him like chattel?" I asked very offendedly.

"You would not be chattel. You would be his."

He turned fully towards me. "The Legion knows that I caused this. They will do anything to prevent the humans from discovering who we are. I am sending you with Eli to protect you."

He felt uncomfortable with this decision but felt that he had to. I nodded sadly.

"If...I should be discovered, they will...execute me."

"You are immortal. How can a human kill you?"

"Not the humans, the Legion. We cannot chance our discovery. They normally execute both the fallen and his chosen, but you...will be protected."

"Why, will I be protected?"

"Because I gave your father and your brother my word that I would."

"You would expect me to be Lord Eli's woman, with his wife, should they discover what you are?"

"It is better this way."

I hugged him sadly. "Let us go into hiding. We can be together." *'I do not know how I would continue on, without feeling your presence. I have gotten so used to feeling you.'* It had become like living. *'I do not know if I could exist without you'.*

"No!" *'I will atone for what li have caused'.*

He climbed on top of me changing the subject. "I want to put my baby inside you."

"Now?" I asked worriedly. That was the last thing on my mind. "Why now?"

"If they should have to kill me, the baby will be my gift to you." He kissed me slowly.

Pushing apart my legs, he joined with me. I felt his every inch as he fought to connect with me completely. He rubbed my sensitive feminine part with his thumb causing me to quiver in his arms. Our breathing quickened and our desires sprang alive stronger. He sucked at my ear. I felt it down there and I groaned. He sucked and kissed at my neck, I groaned louder. He began a low growl. I felt that inside me as it rumbled up and down my spine causing me to shiver below him. I began to move against him closing my eyes, throwing my head back and arching into him.

"Navarhys......!" My body pulsed then I came, convulsing below him.

Navarhys came hard. Changing, he drove himself into me repeatedly with all his might. He arched his back backward howled sexily into the darkness.

Afterward, I held him tightly. I did not want to leave him.

'Nor do I want you to leave.'

I ate breakfast with Navarhys and Tomas in our dining hall. I cried hugging them both. The time for me to leave came too quickly.

Eli stood by our back door expectantly. I busted out crying, clinging to Navarhys. "I do not want to go with him, please Navarhys."

'You promised to obey me Star.' He did not hug me. He stood firm pushing me away from him.

"I also promised not to leave you."

Eli pulled me away from Navarhys forcibly, holding my arms to my side, pulling me towards our back door.

"You do not love me!" I spat

I saw Navarhys look at me, his tears flowed now. "Ta rika me bariti." He started towards me.

"No, you lie!"

Eli let me go. I fell into Navarhys's embrace. I felt his heart and knew that what he said was true. "I do not want to go. Let me stay. Please!"

"You have to go." He signaled Lord Eli to take me.

Once again Lord Eli dragged me away. This time there was no going back. Once through our back door, I found us in another place.

"Where am I?" I screamed disorientated.

"Calm down, Star." Lord Eli held my hand calming me. "We are on my island."

"How?"

"My gift." He smiled down at me. Tahlia stood next to me, suddenly. "Come, I will show you both around.

Chapter Six

Lord Eli was gracious. Tahlia and I stayed in the guest tower. It had five floors. Two of its floors were a part of the main building. The three additional floors were made up of bedrooms and privies. My bedroom was on the tower's third floor. Tahlia took the bedroom above my own.

Our host demanded our presence at every meal. This he said was to ensure that we were safe. Other than that, we were free to explore the island. No-one here knew of me. We were just the guests of Lord Eli.

I learned that many of Eli's guests were his lovers and also that of his wife. Navarhys was correct, Lord Eli and Lady Miarra were extremely amorous beings.

I found that I could read Lord Eli's thoughts just as I could read Navarhys's. This scared me, but he allayed my fears. "It is your natural gift to read the fallen."

Lord Eli told me that there were different types of fallen. He, himself was a healer. Navarhys was a punisher. Miarra imitated shapes of living things. Eli had wings, but Navarhys and Miarra did not.

"Navarhys can heal."

"He can only heal those who do or could mean something to him. I heal anyone."

"I can heal anyone." I challenged.

Lord Eli turned to me grabbing my arm. He read me and saw the incident with the Chi. He reddened instantly baring his teeth, "But you should not use your gifts."   His voice was raised, his eyes blazed red and frightened me.

"What is Andris? I am unable to read him." I looked away abashed, changing the subject.

"Andris, you know about him?"

Eli let go of my arm. He sounded strange and that worried me. "He would be one of those that take on tasks that may be considered distasteful to humans and fallen alike."

I did not ask. I felt fear in the pit of my stomach. Would Andris be the one to kill Navarhys if things did not turn out the way we planned? I hoped not. Navarhys seemed the stronger of the two.

"Why can't I read him?"

"Because…" he looked at me stoically, "…we do not want you contaminated by evil. We need the star child to remain good. He understands this and he blocks you."

"I read him once."

"You touched him!"

"Yes."

"Do not ever reveal what you saw, and do not touch him again!"

Tahlia and I enjoyed visiting the five different beaches, the many hiding places the children and older inhabitants knew, the small lake, a beautiful waterfall, the village, the fisherman wharf, a farm, the animals, some I had never seen before, and the rocks and many caves. I loved Lord Eli's island. What a wonderful place to be. There was no part of the Island off-limits. Crime on the island was nonexistent.

I injured my knee one afternoon attempting to climb down from a cave on the side of a rocky hill. Lord Eli rushed over to me, seeing Tahlia help me hobble into his castle.

"What happened to you?" Lord Eli asked concern etched in his voice.

"I slipped." With Tahlia's help, I hobbled over to a stuffed seat and flopped down on it. I thought of Navarhys. In his arms, he would have helped me heal quickly.

Lord Eli looked into my eyes and knelt at my feet. He placed his hand on my knee and healed my wound and the hurt. "You are not being mindful of your condition Star." His green eyes looked into me. He then placed his hand on my abdomen.

"Please do not do that!" I did not like him or any other man to touch me as my husband should. Bad enough he healed me. At that moment I should have been thankful to Eli, but I resented him.

He eyed me sternly. "I have vowed to protect you. I only sought to see if the unborn suffered any injury. The child needs you to rest!"

I had not said anything to anyone about my pregnancy. I blushed deeply.

"You are confined to the castle and its immediate grounds."

My mouth hung open in shock and disbelief. Now he thinks to speak to me like he was my husband. We have not crossed the line where I would have to consider Eli my mate. "You cannot tell me what to do."

"You promised Navarhys." He replied sternly. "I could just lock you in your room and trust me I would. Would you prefer that?" His eyes changed to a brilliant fiery red.

"No, My Lord Eli." I looked away from him.

"Good. Look at me!"

I looked at him. His eyes changed to their brilliant green. "Your unborn is important to the fallen. They are special beings that usually find themselves in the service of a fallen."

"How so, Lord Eli?"

"Nephilims are what they are called. They have the sight. They see into possible futures. They read minds and help us through difficulties."

"Rawnie is such?"

Lord Eli smiled at me and nodded, "So was your village witch."

I had not thought of Reine in ages. Though my love for her had not diminished. She was there for my mother and me and had given me my name.

"Who did she work for?"

Lord Eli looked at me with a knowing smile. "She looked out for you. The Legion was watchful of you always. We knew of your coming. We did not know that Navarhys's actions would start the unfolding to your coming and the fulfilling of a prophecy."

"A prophesy?"

"In time Star Child."

"Are they not angry at you for aiding us?"

"Navarhys is my ally. We have journeyed a long way together. If he asks it of me, I will assist him." Lord Eli rose and left Tahlia to eat our lunch by ourselves.

"You are pregnant?" Tahlia asked.

I nodded.

"Why, you not tell me?" She asked speaking in the shortened English she uses sometimes.

"I thought I would be back with Navarhys sooner and we'd announce it together."

Tahlia who had made friends on the island began to go out without me. She loved the freedom that this island allotted her. I hoped that she did not plan to stay behind and leave me.

Lord Eli came to sit with me one day as I sat by the side of the fountain in the courtyard of the castle. "Things are progressing slow Star."

"How so, My Lord?"

"The king of Nabu and His Royal Highness Prince Alexander of Lichenia visited. Both agreed that you could not be this star child. Miarra aged you to your late twenties, but Andris says the house is still being watched. We will wait some more."

"Lord Eli, I am kept inside anyway. Can I not return home?"

Lord Eli looked at me sternly. "This is not all about you. We are trying to save Navarhys and ourselves. One wrong move: If someone says something out of place; If they question someone who visits and sees you; all that we have worked for will be undone."

I nodded though disappointed. My heart felt heavy. I wanted to return home. This island's beauty did not stop my longing to be with Navarhys.

"How is it your other two events, the one with the Chi and your slave were not spoken about?"

I pulled the event out of almost everyone's memory."

"Well, what about the braying ass."

"It was a donkey." I looked at him. The distinction did not seem to impress him. "I did not know that I was responsible for what happened to that animal. I did not know I had any gifts. And I surely did not know that I could alter any one's memory."

"Tahlia remembers your other two events."

I wondered where Tahlia was at that very moment. "Tahlia is turned and she keeps my confidence."

"You were not supposed to know how strong you are just because of situations like this."

"I apologize for all the…"

"It is not your doing." He looked at me with his beautiful green eyes. "Navarhys should have heeded his call."

He looked at me again with a spark in his eyes. "We are going visiting, you and I."

I looked at him puzzled.

Eli and I were gone for about a fortnight. He walked between portals. Any doorway or structure that rose from the ground and connected again to the ground was a portal for him to travel to or from. We traveled to the king's castle in Lichenia while the family dined at a gathering of the gentry. We traveled to the castle of King Jenir of Nabu and then to the palace of Prince Adir. I pulled the memory of the star from all who knew about it and those who believed it existed.

We traveled to my village. I saw my parents briefly. We cried, hugged, talked and cried some more. I left them with false memories about the timing of my birth. We journeyed to ten villages surrounding my village. By the time I left those villages my star was viewed as a tale told by older folks to show that any person could be special.

Tahlia, in my absence, had more time to herself. Her curly brown hair grew longer with sun-bleached golden streaks and she looked beautiful. Her smile brightened up any room she entered. I was happy for her but sad at the same time. I feared losing her.

Lord Eli invited Navarhys to his island. He bought Tomas and Tomas's two men. I hugged my brother first. He looked so lovely with his tan. He had been away from his farm longer than he had ever been and was planning to return shortly. He wanted to see me before he began his journey.

Navarhys hugged me so long I thought he would never let me go. I basked in his acceptance.

Lady Miarra and I walked the grounds of the castle. We spoke about my time in her home and she of hers in mine. She was really pleasant and I liked her company. Tahlia interrupted our conversation rushing up to me visibly upset.

"What is it Tahlia?"

She came to hug me, crying.

"Navarhys has ordered me to marry."

Miarra excused herself as I tried to calm my friend.

"Who?"

"Tahlia looked at me. "I am sure he will be good for me."

"Who?"

"Your brother!"

I felt weak in the knees. I sat down on a bench with Tahlia next to me. I thought of what this would mean. She would be thousands of miles away. I probably would see her rarely if ever again. I had hoped that she would be married locally. Navarhys and I never got around to discussing her. My heart felt heavy.

"Tomas is a good man."

"I know." Tahlia agreed.

"Have you met with him?"

“Yes, Star.”

“Do you at least like him?”

“He is nice.”

“We will at least be related by marriage.” I offered.

She smiled bursting out in tears once again. I warmed knowing that she also had wanted to remain close to me.

Chapter Seven

Navarhys and I walked together on the pebbly beach just below the castle on the night before we were to leave. He and I had not done anything romantic for some time. I enjoyed being in his arms with no one and nothing distracting us. We spoke of events that had occurred and I vowed to try not to use my gifts unless necessary.

Our hosts made ready a feast that night. Lord Eli, his wife Lady Miarra, Tomas, his betrothed Tahlia, and Tomas's two men, along with Navarhys and I sat around the feast.

Eli proposed a toast first to Navarhys and me, and our little blessing, then to Tomas and Tahlia. Dinner passed pleasantly. Tahlia, who sat next to me, and I exchanged our sorrow at our imminent parting. I already missed her. She was not journeying back with Navarhys and I. My brother and Tahlia seemed to be getting along nicely.

"You do know, Star, when you return to Nabu city you will be confined to the home." Miarra smiled at me from across the table.

"Why? I do not show yet and we have taken care of the curiosity surrounding me."

She looked at me strangely. "Navarhys's life will depend on you."

I laughed, "Navarhys is an immortal like you."

Miarra looked at me seriously. She was reading me I felt it. Then she looked at Navarhys. "Navarhys, you have not informed her."

I swung around to look a Navarhys. "What?"

He looked a little shamefaced.

"What have you not told me?"

Navarhys reached for my hand. "I should have told you. I did not want you to worry."

"What?"

'I lose my immortality once you give birth.'

Every open door in the castle slammed shut. The sounded reverberating around us.

Pulling my hand from his, I stood up raging at him. "How could you not tell me that?"

He reached for my hand, but I moved away before he touched me. "You do not like me! I am still just your slave." The castle shook, I heard items crashing to the ground.

"Stop her Navarhys!" Miarra yelled.

Navarhys engulfed me within his arms just before I blacked out.

I lay in Navarhys's arms when I woke. We were in my bed in Nabu. His sandy colored eye regarded me sadly.

"I am sorry Star."

I tried to wiggle out of his arms.

"Star, forgive me please."

I still struggled.

"I do love you Star," he attempted to kiss me.

"Do not do that and please do not say those words."

He released me and moved away from me. He looked sad and hurting. I turned my back to him, but I felt his sadness within me.

We did not exchange words for close to a week. That week felt like an eternity. During that time my sadness increased as I got sicker. Maybe it was his sadness I felt or maybe both our hearts were breaking.

My skin took on a deeper hue of red as I became sicker. Morning sickness was neither kind nor forgiving.

I watched in horror as my pale skin turned an unnatural scarlet red, one morning. Rachel, my new handmaiden, took one look at me, turned and rushed out of my room screaming. Navarhys came, I was too sick to protest his embrace. His closeness felt instantly satisfying. My color returned and my stomach settled.

"I love you," he whispered in my ear.

I, being stubborn, did not respond.

"Hold me, please!" He pleaded, looking into my eyes.

I did not. It was his fault that I was the way I am.

The next time the sickness took a hold of me, he did not come. He felt me. I could feel him. I refused to beg him to help me. I sent Rachel away so I could suffer alone. The awful feeling lasted until the afternoon. Rachel bought me lunch. I accepted it but was in no mood to eat. Food also bought on my sickness.

I went onto our roof to smell the ocean breeze and feel the warming sun on my face. I bought a Tarkarian book with me. I still did not know all the words, but I liked to practice with easy books. Rachel, born a slave, to slave parents did not know how to read.

I felt isolated and alone in this big city of Nabu. My heart ached for Lichenia and that small village of my childhood. There I was never alone.   There I knew my brother Tommie and my mother loved me. I still did not have that faith in Navarhys despite what he said and all that he had done.

In bed that night my stomach cried and ached with hunger. The next day I woke sick. My stomach heaved on emptiness. I cried silently and wished that I was not special. I wished with all my heart that I was just an ordinary human girl with an ordinary life.

Rawnie found me heaving, weak and doubled over by my bedside. She ran out to find my handmaiden and Navarhys.

I heard her reprimanding Rachel. "I do not care what she told you, your duty is to be with her!" "Get some fresh water and prepare some clean clothes and bedding."

Navarhys enter soon afterward.

"Navarhys, how could you let Star suffer like this?" Rawnie could barely hold in her anger. "It is no wonder she does not feel that you love her."

"She does not want me."

"Navarhys! Open your eyes, she needs you."

Brahada entered carrying a warm bowl of soup. Rawnie took it from her. "Come Star." I sat up determined, not wanting to disappoint Rawnie. I tried to keep it down, but I soon lost my natural color, turned scarlet and erupted.

Navarhys came to me then. I felt the crush of his arms around me. He pulled me to sit on his lap.

"Why did you not call me?"

I heaved once again. I could have pointed out that he knew because he could feel all that I experienced, but I did not. "I am sorry," I uttered weakly. Sorry that I had gotten so angry with him, sorry for the hurtful words that I spoke to him, sorry for the bad state that I was in now, and sorry for causing Rawnie to have to speak to him about me.

I needed him so badly. The tears burned in my eyes.

"I will treat you better, I promise." He vowed, sinking his head into the nook between my shoulder and head. "Allow me to feed you."

My stomach growled just by me hearing his words. I was so hungry. Navarhys fed me and spoke to me. The room emptied. He admitted that he should have told me the significance of this pregnancy. He revealed to me that he knew when I was badly hurt by the donkey because for the first time in his existence he laid in bed in severe pain. He became aware that I was slipping away, and he reached out to me in my dreams. He describes the event as, "...our soul reconnecting..."

"Your life would be easier with Aeyden."

He looked at me for a long moment. Sadness hung about him like a cloak. "I will not punish you for not being her. I have tried to do right by you but not love you.   I find cannot help myself. What I do know is, you cannot hurt me as she as hurt me."

"You mean I cannot die and leave you behind."

He looked sadly at me again, scooping more soup into me. He continued with his story. He told me how he kept an eye on me after the accident.   He would visit me in my dreams periodically. Reine kept the Legion informed of me also. Rawnie informed him just before he finally came to claim me. She said that if he did not leave and soon, I would be married. He also informed me that my pregnancy intensified my gifts and that I could become very dangerous and deadly without being fully aware of it.   My gifts were to be used for protection only, especially of my children. During my pregnancy, I had to be confined for everyone's safety as well as my own.

Before I knew it, I had eaten all the soup.   Navarhys prevented my sickness. We snuggled together below the sheets, though it must not have been pleasant for him. I still had not washed the vomit off myself.

"I have located Xio."

"Really!"

"He works on a merchant ship. I have sent word to let him know that he is invited to visit when next he is in port."

"What of the one who owns him?"

"I have taken care of that."

"Tell me, what is it you have done?"

"I paid for the return of his papers."

"But by you paying for the return of his paper, are you not telling him that you are guilty in Xio's disappearance?"

"For what I gave him, he would not mention Xio, ever."

"So, you own him again?"

"I suppose so, but I would not act on it, because I know that would displease you."

"May I have them?"

"Yes." He kissed me.

I smiled snuggling close to him.

My morning sickness became easier to endure now that Navarhys paid more attention to me.

After my morning sickness had abated, Navarhys replaced Rachel with an older woman. She came with the knowledge of birthing and babies. Between Rawnie and my new slave, Miriam, I had plenty of mothering.

Miriam, a Christian, captured in raids then sold to slavers of this country. I saw her devotion and wanted to know more. She began to tell me about Christianity.

"Please Star. I need you," he whispered in my ear.

I fought sleep. The unborn wore heavily on me. "I am tired." I kissed him. "I will...when the sun rises." I moved my face away from his.

His hands crept up my clothing capturing breasts.

"Now," he pleaded. "I want you."

He pulled my nightclothes up taking my breast fully into his mouth. His tongue flickering back and forth as he suckled me. He pressed himself against me hard.

"Navarhys I..."

He began sinking into me slowly, moaning with pleasure. I could not resist opening for him, signally my sweet surrender. He looked at me, his sandy eyes aglow with candle lights.

"Ta rika me bariti." He kissed me first tenderly then he became more and more demanding.

We began to do our lovemaking dance; every movement taking us deeper into our emotional world. I moan his name into his ear. He changed from his human guise to his big hard hot authenticity. He could not help but growl as his progress neared completion. Enchanted I felt my body release, losing composure. His hardness inside me shuddered. I clung to his hands and feet, wanting him with me always.

"Ta rika me bariti," he repeated.

"I love you too."

His bite on my neck took me by surprise. Instead of pulling away, I bared more of myself to him. He sucked on my blood. Spent he laid beside me holding me.

I lay facing Navarhys feeling very content. Although I was sure I would not get any sleep, our active unborn moved within me and kicked at me with vigor. I moved Navarhys's hand to my abdomen. His eyes looked at me with such tenderness. My heart expanded with gratitude.

"Ta rika me bariti," he whispered to me through the darkness.

"Always?"

"Forever!" He pulled me close, kissing me just behind my ear.

I squealed giggling pushing him away playfully. *'You are not helping my slumber.'*

He looked at me in that way that took my breath away. His big hands caressed my stomach. *'I love you Star.'* He moved my head, so I again looked into his eyes, *'You believe me?'*

'Yes, I believe you.' I moved his hand back to my tummy placing my hands on top his.

Navarhys rose and kiss my expanded middle. "Sleep little one, your mama needs her rest." The unborn's movements slowed.

Smiling handsomely, he pulled me into his arms. *'Sleep, my love...'*

Be careful what you wish for, that is what my mother told me growing up. At the time her comments were directed at the mysterious man with orange yellowy eyes, I would not let go of. That mysterious man, Navarhys, now would not let go of me.

The only thing special on the day my Elyan was born was his birth. I liked it that way. My cries kept everyone away except the ones who cared. Navarhys, Rawnie, Miarra, and Miriam. They all cared for me during my twelve hours of labor. Navarhys suffered with me. At first, I thought that he was making fun of me. I quickly realized that my pains were his. My admiration and love for him blossomed deeper.

They tried to hide it from me, but I heard them talking, the house was still being watched on occasion. Navarhys doubted that it was by the crown, but they were not sure by whom.

Navarhys added Miriam's cot to my room for the time being. He gave me more skins, purchased off the merchant ships. I hung some of the prettier ones on my walls and used a few to separate Miriam and little Elyan's cradle from my bed. I slept better not seeing him. On my wall, he hung two paintings of and from my county, Lichenia. I also began to get letters from my family. These letters were like feeling the essence of those that I love and miss dearly.

Little Elyan was so dear to me. I loved him more than I loved myself. I could not bear to hear him cry. Miriam proved to be a knowledgeable slave. She had answers for my every inquiry and knew what Elyan needed at his every whimper. My letters back to my family were full of his worship. Navarhys adored our son also. He came each night to hold him or just to watch Elyan's perfect little features.

Navarhys would not allow me to move about the house freely until Elyan reached eight weeks of age. Nor did he allow anyone to visit.

The head of the local church stopped by a few times to visit and bless the baby, but Navarhys would not allow him near Elyan or me.

"This man thinks he has a right to demand to see my babe because he is a man of God," Navarhys sneered. "I know God more than he possibly could."

"Do you not think he would find it strange of you to keep him away?"

"I do not attend his church. He can think whatever he wants to."

I wondered why the official would come knowing that we did not attend his church. Nabu being a city of many religions, did not even know what religion if any we practiced.

Navarhys's features did not fail to soften whenever he looked down at his sleeping son.

I loved them so very much. I was happy when Elyan turned two months old and my husband lifted my confinement. Now I had the privilege of the house.

On that very first day that I was granted more freedom, I felt his need the entire evening beginning at supper. I walked into our dining hall. He had already begun to dine. Lord Eli dined with him.

Lord Eli stood and inclined his head in my direction. "Greetings Star." Navarhys greeted me with a kiss to the corner of my lips. "You look lovely Star."

"Thank you Navarhys."

While they made conversation, I ate quietly. Every time I looked towards Navarhys, his eyes were upon me. I felt my whole body heat up sexually.

'You are embarrassing me!'

'Eli knows what we are about.'

'You do not have to make it so obvious.'

'Trust me, the things we do are tame compared to Eli and his wife.'

I blushed brightly seeing the laughter playing on Eli's lips.

"You should not read our private thoughts, Lord Eli."

'My humblest apologies Star.'   I read his thought, but the smile did not leave his lips.

I bathed, nursed Elyan and Miriam put him to bed, then retired to her cot on the other side of my room.

Navarhys entered my room naked. The red-tinged already stained his skin. I awaited him naked on the top of my bedspreads. My body tingled at the sight of him.

He changed, feeling my need for him. In response, I burned to feel his touch. He proceeded towards me swiftly capturing my hips in his arms. For the first time, I felt his tongue on my feminine organ. His tongue inflamed my desires and shivers of need rippled through my stomach. I moaned wantonly, grabbing his head with one hand holding him there. With my other hand, I grabbed onto the sheets arching my back, this coupling almost felt too overwhelming. Breathing and moaning heavily, tossing from side to side, I could not hold it any longer my body released wave after wave of overwhelming euphoria. Navarhys, now the giant red being, sunk into me roaring lustfully. His crimson hard hot body moved about me and inside of me pushing the boundaries of lust already conquered. I welcomed his every need, matching the sexual torment that left us both needing more.

"Navarhys….!"

I found myself in darkness, alone. The only sound I heard was the sound of my frightened heart. I called out for Navarhys. My voice died in the darkness. I tried to feel around. There was nothing. I listened. In the distance, I heard my baby's cry. I called out for my husband again. There was still no reply. "Where are you?" I yelled crying. "I need you!"

I heard laughter. It was coming closer to me. My heart thundered in my ears. Though I had never heard it before. I knew whose laughter it was, Andris.

I woke to find that Navarhys had spilled his seed on top of my stomach. "Do not look!" he growled menacingly with red glowing eyes. "Why did you push me away?"

"I did?" I again tried to look down.

Navarhys growled at me, turning red and baring his sharpened teeth. He grabbed the sheets and wiped his semen away. Anger ruled his movements.

"I am sorry. I was dreaming. I did not realize that I pushed you out." I tried to make eye contact, but he would not.

He rose, finished with his task, without saying another word. He took the soiled sheets with him to his room.

I remained in my room wondering what the dream had meant. 'Me, in that immense *blackness, alone.*'

The next morning, I did what I had not dared to do in the past, I went to Navarhys's room. He lay on top of his sheets in his changed form. When I had seen him asleep in the past, he never slept in that form. I boldly climbed on his bed. He stirred, opening his eyes. I reached towards him, but he intercepted my hand. He moved to a sitting position on the bed. Just before he took me, I saw his full erection. I was not ready, but I did not utter a sound of protest. He picked me up then repeatedly pulled me onto him. His body retained its crimson color, but his eyes reflected a beautiful golden tone. I felt him holding my heart in those eyes. He kissed me as he erupted inside of me.

Laying me gently on his bed, he looked down on me. He lay his hand on my abdomen. I felt his hand heat up and my abdomen also.

"What are you doing?"

"Ensuring that you are carrying."

"So soon," I complained.

"I am protecting you."

"From what?"

He kissed me and we made love, this time he was the Navarhys that showered me with his tender touch and loving affection.

Rawnie visited on a pleasantly warm day. The curtains of my room billowed softly in the mid-morning breeze allowing amble sunlight into my bedroom. My room had changed in the few weeks since Elyan's birth.

She smiled contently, "He treats you better?"

"Yes," I answered with a smile. Miriam held Elyan while Rawnie and I talked.

"I am glad he replaced Rachel."

"So am I," I stated smiling with Miriam as she rocked my son to sleep.

Rawnie and I sat on one of my long-stuffed chairs. I asked Miriam to get one of the slaves to fetch us something to eat and a drink for each of us.

Rawnie reached into her pouch, she retrieved three small differently colored leather-covered balls. She shook each one. Each, slightly different in size, made a different sound.

"Thank you Rawnie. I am sure he will love them when he is a little older."

"That he will" she agreed, holding my hand.

I hugged her thankful that she was my friend. Right then I needed the feel of another. If I had been back home, it would have been my mother. I would have her guidance, not Miriam's and I would have her comfort instead of Rawnie's. I missed my mother. I made a mental note to put that in the next letter I wrote to her.

Just then I heard a quick knock, followed by Andris bursting into my room.

"What are you doing here?" I asked annoyed and afraid at the same time. He never came to me let alone entered my room. I hardly exchanged words with him despite the length of time we spent under the same roof.

"Forgive me Star," he bowed at my knee and reached for my hand kissing it. "I...we are urgently in need of your help."

"Who?"

"They need you to clear the mind of a child." He explained to me that Lord Eli and Lady Miarra's arrival was imminent and with them, they have a Nephilim girl. Her parents had been executed by the Legion. Her knowledge of which will traumatize her future. They needed me to remove the knowledge she had of the execution."

"Why were they executed?"

He looked at me with burgundy eyes, "To hide our existence."

My heartbeat quickened. "Where is Navarhys?"

"Star, we have no time. She will arrive with Lord Eli and Lady...." He stopped and inclined his head. "They are here." He turned back to me. His eyes were now an intense bright red. "Do it now before she senses your presence and intentions!"

I felt her deep loss, anger, and resentment. I saw what she had seen, and I cried. I pulled the memory as soon as I saw it and replaced it with what Andris wanted. He still held my hand. He wanted the child to think her parents were burned at the stake by the humans for being witches. I could not see how that would be less traumatizing, but then in her new reality, the fallen saves her.

Andris looked at me as if for the first time. I felt his admiration and felt embarrassed. "Thank you, Star, the Legion will not forget."

Again, fear stirred in the pit of my stomach. While he held my hand, I learned what type of demon he was: a terminator and torturer. He was sinful and immoral. He did not wish to become enlighten or to ascend. I also learned that he had killed Aeyden. He had infected her with a drop of his lethal fluids earlier on in the day that she had died. It had slowly killed her. The legion had ordered it so that Navarhys would acknowledge me, his Chosen. Navarhys could not see this, nor could Rawnie, but I saw.

After he left, I noticed that Rawnie did not seem like her normal jovial self.

"What is the matter Rawnie?" I asked, seeing how unusually pale she now seemed.

"The next time one of *them* asks you to do them a favor, insist that Navarhys is with you," she bristled. "Your gifts are to be used in the defense of you and your family, especially for your offspring."

I turned and held her hand. "Did I do something wrong?"

"Do not let anyone ask you to use any of your gifts without Navarhys being with you. You used the gift that is most powerful and who were you defending? Be careful, for you will throw the balance of forces off."

I felt that something else ate at her and saw it in a flash. She pulled away from me realizing my intrusion.

"You know and saw what ails me!" She retorted, looking at me with anger in her eyes.

I nodded. If they did as you suspect, they still looked out for you. Leaving you with gypsies protected you. Your gifts would not be accepted in most other communities."

"I want to know if I am truly alone in this world, or if I have a family. My human parent may have relatives. I would like to know them."

Feeling at odds with Rawnie, I felt defensive toward the fallen. "Your gypsy clan is your family. That is all you have ever known."

"You know that I speak of blood."

"I know." I agreed, turning away from her. Knowing that I could not bear to see into another execution if that is what had happened to her parents. I asked insincerely, "Would you like for me to inquire?"

Just then Navarhys entered my room. He came to me, kissed me on my cheek. When he looked into my eyes, I revealed only that which had occurred with the child.

"You have been crying.

I nodded.

He turned to Rawnie, "Please excuse us."

Rawnie replied, "I was just leaving." She still did not sound herself. "Good day to you both."

I went to kiss her cheeks, as she held my hands, I pulled the memory of what had transpired since Andris came to my room.

"Good day, my friend." I smiled

Rawnie smiled back, happy.

"Miriam, take your leave, now," Navarhys ordered.

I looked at my husband and saw the worry on his handsome face. A heaviness took hold in the pit of my stomach. "What is it Navarhys?"

"We are still in danger. The child spoke of it before she arrived here."

I hugged him. "Maybe she is wrong. Rawnie had not said anything."

He hugged me placing his chin on top of my head. "A Nephilim child is untainted with feelings of friendship and allegiances. Rawnie looks to you like a mother looks to her child. She will see, but she will see too late.

He looked into my eyes, "Did Rawnie tell you that she knew her daughter would die?"

I shook my head.

"She knew the moment she begged me to save Aeyden. Rawnie knew our happiness would be short-lived, but she said nothing."

"Why?"

Navarhys shrugged, "She wanted more time with her daughter. Maybe she wanted her daughter to be happy."

I looked at his face and still saw the pain of his loss.

"It made no difference if her daughter left the house that night or not, she would have died."

"I am sorry for your loss Navarhys."

"Please my love, listen to me." He embraced me. "We are in danger. The child wishes to speak to you. You must listen."

"As you wish." A vivid image flashed in my thoughts; Andris beheading of the child's father witnessed by both the child and her mother. The child and her mother wailing for their beloved and the fear within them as Andris pursued them. Andris beheaded the mother also. The fallen parent was just as mortal as her human parent at that point. The beheadings were not necessary. He could have killed them in a less traumatic way and without the child's presence. He was a cruel being.

"Clear your mind quickly," Navarhys read my thoughts. "She can read you."

I turned to him tears flooding out of my eyes, "If I die, you die also. But if you die. I do not."

"Yes," he kissed me again. "It is as it is."

"I do not want you to protect me. If they come to execute you, I want to journey with you."

"You wish to die with me? Elyan will need you."

"Eli and Miarra would look out for him."

"Speak of this no more. I have made my decision."

"I want to be with you always." I cried.

"If you love me Star, you will abide my wishes."

"I felt sorrow and an overwhelming sadness seep in my core.

Navarhys felt it too. "I know   you love me." He kissed me gently. "I know you have loved me from the very beginning. I cannot punish others, then run and hide when it is my turn. Honor my wishes!"

I sobbed because I could not bear to think of life without him. I know I would be hopelessly lost. Without a doubt, my feelings for him would dwarf his lingering feelings for Aeyden. I knew I would be blanketed in my grief.

Miarra came to my room soon after Navarhys left. The child moved silently behind her.

"Greetings Star. I have someone who wants to meet with you."

Wiping my tears, I welcomed my friend. "Greetings, Lady Miarra. It is so lovely to meet with you again, and who is this?" I gestured towards the brown-haired little girl tailing her.

"This is Granoal. My Lord husband and I are fostering her."

"Greetings, Granoal. How are you?"

"Fine, thank you, and yourself?" Her voice sounded sweet and bell-like. She looked up at me with big owl-like eyes.

"Is there something that you would like to tell me little one?"

She nodded reaching out for my hand.

"I am like your son."

"I know," I replied.

"They know about you."

"Who does?"

"The church."

"The church?" My heart felt like it had dropped to the pit of my stomach.

"How?"

"They notice any changes in the heavens. They know who you are, but they do not yet know what Navarhys is. We must wipe the knowledge of you from their minds. Protection of the fallen is very important."

"What would happen if the fallen are discovered?"

"An insidious War." Her big owl eyes looked up at me. "The church against whom they think may be a fallen. From a distance, you cannot tell who is good, who is bad. The church in its belief that all fallen must be erased, will kill humans and fallen alike. The fallen know the difference between themselves and men. Human-kind will be bought to near extinction."

"We cannot let that happen."

"No, we cannot." Granoal agreed with a smile.

We were leaving my bedroom when Granoal held my hand once again. She turned towards me. "You have the gift to change everything."

Miriam approached us.   "Elyan is fussing, he needs you, ma'am."

I smiled hurrying to the roof. When we got there, Navarhys, Lord Eli and Lady Miarra with Elyan were lounging around drinking wine and speaking in hushed voices.

Miarra looked my way with Elyan in her arms. He was truly beginning to fuss for his feeding. My breast filled with milk just hearing him.

Navarhys came towards me kissing me lightly on the side of my lips.

"Ta rika me bariti."

I blushed because everyone heard. He sounded so sexy. "Ta rika me bariti, da." I pulled away. Elyan needed me. I took him out of Lady Miarra's arms, sat down at a nearby bench and started nursing him.

Miarra sat down next to me. "Did she tell you?"

She meant Granoal. "She did."

"We need you strong."

"You need me pregnant," I replied knowing now why Navarhys got so angry with me the night before and why he was not initially so giving this morning. I looked towards Navarhys. He looked at me smiling, whilst in the midst of his conversation with Lord Eli.

'You are so beautiful.'

'That is new. You have not said that before.' His words did not make me feel soft inside. His words made me feel fear.

Chapter Eight

That night as we lay in Navarhys's bed, he recited a poem to me in his native tongue. The poem told a story about a lost disembodied soul wandering the dunes of a desert in search of a place to rest.

They came and I had not heard or felt them come. "It is time."

I sprang up frightened by the closeness of the voice. I knew what they were once I lay eyes on them.

"I cannot leave you," I turned to Navarhys bawling and clinging to him. "I promised to stay with you."

"Star, do as they say," Navarhys whispered in my ear. He hugged me and I blacked out.

I came to, sitting in a big chair facing three fallen. The same three that had visited with Navarhys at an earlier time. I still wore my nightclothes; my feet were bare on the cold stone floors. We sat in a large cavernous hall with vaulted ceilings. Lanterns hung from the pillars casting moving shadows of light and darkness. The place felt eerie to me. The fallen in the middle looked aged, long white wispy hair, a thin face. A face made to look longer because of his long thin beard. The one to the right was handsome with black hair, olive skin, deep-set searching eyes, and a hook nose. The woman sat to the left. She looked regal wearing a fine blue dress trimmed with lace. Her auburn hair held back in a bun. She had blue piercing eyes and a tanned complexion.

"Where is my husband?" I demanded angrily.

The three fallen sitting in their throne-like chairs looked stoically back at me in silence.

"Why is he not here?"

Still, they said nothing. I decided to follow by example. Finally, the female asked, "Do you know why you are?"

Silence.

"We shall tell you." The youngest looking one stated. "Navarhys neglected his duty to immediately claim you, his chosen. In doing so, he has provided a doorway for humans to discover us. Luck seems to be on his side, we have recently learned of your unusual gift."

He paused expectantly. I remained silent.

"With your gift, we can erase all knowledge of your unusual star. Then once again we can live at ease."

"Where is Navarhys?"

The eldest spoke. "Ahelia we need your help."

"I cannot feel Navarhys. What have you done to him?" Tears swelled in my eyes. I felt lost, without our souls being joined.

"Maybe you need to rest. We shall speak later."

Another fallen was summoned into the hall to escort me to my quarters. He showed me to a huge room with a four-poster bed off to the side. The room had elaborate paneling. A huge painting of war between demons and men hung on one wall. On the opposite wall, an oversized painting hung off me. Around the bed, the burgundy rug felt warm below my feet. This room lit by lamps appeared welcoming though it had no windows.

The door clicked lock behind me as walked further into the room, my fallen escort gone.

I went to the bed and lay down on top of the sheets. I did not want to feel comfortable in this windowless prison. I did not know what time of the day it was, and I could not feel Navarhys. I closed my eyes trying to find him. It allowed me a little solace to drift off to a troubled sleep.

A fallen awakened me; the youngest one of the three from earlier.

"Greetings, Ahelia. My name is Maxen."

"Where is my husband?" I had not slept well because I still could not feel Navarhys and it left me terrified. I felt so lost and lonely. I could barely remember a time when I could not at least feel his presence. I felt like I was missing a part of me that was vital to my life.

"We have not harmed your husband."

"Why is he not here?"

"We only need you."

"You are lying. You have done something to him." I burst into tears. "I cannot feel him."

"I give you my word, we have not harmed Navarhys."

"I want him bought here."

"After you have complied with our request."

"I will not do anything you ask of me unless my husband is with me."

"You showed your gift willingly to Andris when he asked."

I thought about his statement and remembered Rawnie's warning. "If I had known that the Legion had been testing me, I would have declined. Surely you have a fallen that could have done what I did. I will not use my gifts simply because you ask it of me."

"Your baby is in need of his mother."

My breast filled at the mention of my son. I looked at Maxen with pure hatred.

"Do you see the paintings we have on the walls?" He walked over to the one baring my image.

I did not respond.

"This one of you was painted two centuries ago by a child-like your son."

Though impressed, I still did not respond. I looked at the painting and it was definitely me.

"We knew you would come. We know you will help us prevent what the other painting depicts."

"Or maybe I will cause it."

A flicker of fear flashed in his eyes.

"Bring me, my husband."

"If you refuse to assist us, I will harm Elyan."

I looked away from him. I could not stand to look upon him any longer. My blood felt like it was boiling within my body. I heard his struggle to breathe, and his fall to the ground. Just then, the door to my prison flew open and in rushed five fallen.

"Stop this Ahelia!" The female fallen from earlier demanded in a high-pitched voice. "He only said that to convince you to aid us."

"Bring me my Navarhys!"

"First, release him."

"He is an immortal, a few missing breaths of stale air will not harm him." In the few moments it took for her to answer, I read her desperate thoughts. I learned that I had the ability to kill them and not merely by beheading. I could make them suffer because Navarhys was a punisher and I was a part of him. I immediately cleared my mind.

"Stop!" It was the elder of the original trio. He raised his palm towards me and pushed the air forcefully towards me. I felt a cool breeze brush around me, then rebounded back the way it came. The ancient flew back towards the door bouncing off its frame.

'She is pregnant...She carries Navarhys's seed......She is with child again...We are harmless against her.'

I heard their thoughts. Navarhys had truly protected me. They could not hurt me while I carried.

The ancient stumbled to his feet and once again came towards me. This time he came humbly. "Please Ahelia, we will bring you Navarhys. He turned and spat out a few words in an ancient tongue. Then back to me, "Release Maxen. Navarhys is coming."

With my thoughts alone, I flung Maxen against a wall, released my invisible stranglehold on his throat, but held him immobilized. Unable to hold his human form any longer Maxen changed into a purple demon.

"How long must I wait?" I asked growing angrier, my skin turning an unnatural red. My world was closing in on me. The outer fringes of my vision darkening.

I saw my love enter through the portal alongside Eli. Our soul connected before I went running into his embrace. "You are whole!" I sobbed loudly. My body once again felt rejuvenated. The darkness that had begun to encircle me receded into nothing.

"Yes Star," he held me tight.

"You knew they meant to execute you."

"I am sorry my love." He kissed me on my forehead as he held me tightly in his hug.

"You knew what my dream meant." I accused him, tearfully.

"Yes, I knew."

"Why did you not tell me?"

"I hate to see you worry," he whispered in my ear.

"I can save you," I whispered back.

"Release me!" Maxen demanded irritated at his continued restraint.

Without looking his way, I complied.

"Kill them both!" Maxen shouted at the slowly enlarging gathering of the Legion.

He lived just long enough to feel his body being ripped opened from his abdomen and to see his entails drop before him to the ground. My face was the last image he saw in this world. His remains disintegrated completely as if he had never existed.

"Star!" Eli yelled shocked.

I looked at him and saw as he changed sprouting his magnificent wings he went down on his knee. The others followed also changing and acquiesce to their knees.

"He threatened me. He threatened my family."

The ancient one spoke. "We humbly ask that you remove all knowledge of your star from the minds of those who saw."

"I have already done that."

"Some remain,"

"What of the written knowledge, who will alter that?" Navarhys asked placing his arm protectively around me. I looked at him with a smile.

The ancient addressed him. "We have placed fallen strategically to alter the written evidence and all the important text as of this night will be gone."

"What is special about tonight?" I asked.

"The blue comet will streak across our skies. It has been said that your powers will be greater. We are also fortunate that you are carrying. Your gift will be exponentially..."

I raised my hand for him to stop talking. "You," I pointed to a fallen that kneeled just off to the left of the ancient. He had flaxen hair, deep blue eyes, and a pale complexion. I had not noticed him before, but his thoughts had seeped through my conversation with the ancient. "What is your name?"

"I am named Jancov..."

"I want you to approach us."

Nervously he rose to his feet and did as I commanded. "You convinced the counsel to deal harshly with my husband?"

"I...I..."

"You also threatened my family."

"Star, do not do this." Eli pleaded beside me still on his knee.

"Do what, Eli?" I asked resentfully.

"Do not punish him...or worse."

"What do you think Navarhys?" I asked turning to my beloved.

He looked into my eyes. "I have punished fallen for much less than what I have caused. He did what he was supposed to do. He should not be punished."

"Barniursius," I called to the ancient. I had pulled his name from his thoughts. "I want your word my husband will not be harmed."

"You have my word." He looked at me expectantly. He wanted me to beg him not to harm me.

"Good." I stated then to the gathering, "Please leave me with my husband, all of you. Lord Eli, you stay."

"Star, you trod on dangerous territory. The fallen are vengeful. They will come after you."

"If they remember they will."

Lord Eli looked at me with new eyes. He did not think that I could alter the thoughts of a fallen.

"Star," Navarhys looked into my eyes. "I do not wish to be cut off from the Legion."

"They wanted to execute you," I stated angrily.

He held both my hands within his, "I do not want to be apart from them."

"I only wish to protect you the way you sought to protect Aeyden. I don't want anything to befall you."

"Star!" Lord Eli interrupted me. "Navarhys does not wish it."

I looked towards Lord Eli and he regarded me with a look of warning. *'We cannot harm you now, but Navarhys still can. He is your balance.'*

I looked towards my Navarhys. He could but I knew that he would not. "I am sorry Navarhys."   I hugged him feeling his deep hurt at the words I spoke. "I am sorry. Do you forgive me?"

"Yes, my love," he whispered kissing me on the top of my head. He warmed to me and I felt it.

I vowed to myself never to mention Aeyden again unless he did so first. Navarhys hugged me tightly. I felt his smile along my cheek. "You are a goddess."

I giggled, "You say that because you want me to say that you are a god."

Chapter Nine

The ancient stones hidden deep within a dormant volcano allowed for contact throughout the earth.

Navarhys put me to sleep and took me to the secret sacred place. Many lanterns lit our way.   They, the fallen, escorted us into a cavern leading to the heart of the dormant volcano. At that place, all the fallen showed their true selves. I saw small, medium, and large fallen in a variety of colors. Some of the Legion had wings but many did not. I saw that Eli's wings were magnificent compared to many and he was among the larger few. I noted that some fallen changed in stages, my Navarhys changed in two.

The stones were not stones, they were huge dark gray rocks that looked like they had tried to escape the red earth around them. The fallen bowed and kneeled to me as we passed them. They hummed and beat on their chest rhythmically.

We walked up to Barniursius, the ancient. He too kneeled but looked at me as he spoke. "It has been said that you, Ahelia, would prevent a worldwide catastrophe. That fallen and humans will continue to live alongside one another for thousands of years. It has been said that you are a benevolent being."

I nodded.

"The comet will be visible in a few moments."

Navarhys squeezed my hand tighter. I turned towards him and smiled. He looked like his giant red self and radiated that heat that he does when he transforms. With his other hand, he placed my other hand on one of the warm gray monoliths. The blue light from the comet appeared to shower down from the old volcano's opening above. Its light crept over my hand and covered me.

Navarhys whispered in my ear, "You are glowing, my beautiful Star".

I was, and so were the stones.

Barniursius uttered urgently, "Now Star rob them of their knowledge."

Many faces flashed in my mind: old faces, younger faces, men, and women. I finally saw my star through their eyes and what a wondrous sight she was. I smiled seeing my parents, my brothers, and the people of my village and the villages surrounding mine.   I saw laymen, Sheppard, clergy, spies, stargazers, soldiers, and many more. The witnesses to my star were plentiful. I pulled the memory of my star from all but my brother Tommie, who treasured it, Navarhys, whose actions had begun the unfolding of a prophecy, Rawnie, whose daughter died as the star became visible to mortals and the legion. I pulled the thought of retribution against me from the clan. I pulled the lingering sadness about Aeyden from Navarhys's heart, replacing his sadness with contentment at having been a good friend, lover, and provider for her. Before I removed my hand and before the comet's light disappeared, I uttered the words that Miriam had taught me, "May there be peace on earth and goodwill towards men."

Many of our days were happy and my Navarhys was content. Our twins, the girl Nya and the boy Namus were born on a sunny day. Navarhys found another guard for me. He allowed me for short spells out of the house and into the gated quarter if my guard accompanied me. Beyond the gated quarter, I was only allowed there if Navarhys accompanied me because Navarhys was the only fallen that could check me and my abilities should I ever lose control. As stated, the people outside of the gated quarter were not as civilized as those that lived inside the gated community.

I am a rare Chosen for I know I had immense powers. The Legion did not trust that I could contain my gifts if circumstances arose. Part of their creed was for a fallen to claim their chosen as soon as it was possible. They are then charged with convincing their Chosen that they were not powerful because one; it throws off the balance, and two; one's belief is a power greater than any gift or liberty.

Spirit, The Unborn

Chapter One

Adbent

Etan feared cold moonless nights like these. Beyond the torch's illumination, shadows danced and played tricks on his eyes.

Sounds of horses neighing and shuffling hooves made this boy's heart and playful mind conjure stories of hidden menaces peering back at him from beyond the darkness.

Hay poked at him; his ragged clothes providing no shield. Closing his eyes and cowering below his threadbare horse blanket, tempered his fears. He should be walking around to ensure the safety of the king's remaining horses, but his fears on this dark night increased with each sound and each moving shadow. Etan crouched in a corner, certain that he'd hear if any of the soldiers returned to check on him. Another stable boy also scheduled to keep watch of the stables, had fallen ill.

The other stable hands slept snugly in their cots to await the king and his companions. Still, the remaining horses needed to be kept safe from thieves and hungry serfs.

From the darkness, the sound of the wind howling, brought to mind, a widow in mourning.

Pulling rough coarse material tighter around him, Etan cringed more frightened than ever. His heart raced soundly within him.

A sudden loud ear-splitting boom sounded close, rocking the earth below him. He almost jumped out of his skin.

Around him, the stables lit brightly.

Horses whined in terror; kicking at their stalls. Etan screamed grabbing his prickly blanket ever closer. Winds howled as if in pain. Then darkness. So dark, Etan saw and felt the blackness though he held his eyes tightly closed.

He opened them and noticed that he did not hear a sound; no beast or wind, nothing.

'Was that smoke,' he thought to himself, scenting the smell.

From the darkness, Etan thought he heard a cat cry. Then the horses began their worried whinnying again.

"Quiet you dumb beasts." Etan's voice sounded inadequate, choking on fear. He stood against a wall. Coughing, he realized that smoke burned at his eyes and clouded his lungs. He then saw flames through the darkness. Black shadows of frantic horses played against bright dancing flames.

Just as he was about to raise the alarm, he heard others yell, "Fire! Fire!"

"Fire," Etan yelled running to the closest stall unaided by his torch. Feeling along rough wooden planks, he unlatched the gate. A frightened colt and its mare pushed open the gate as they rushed past him, knocking him to his knees. He heard a faint out of place sound. He felt his way to the next gate and unlocked that one also. Thick smoke stung his eyes blinding him and burning his lungs, but Etan continued feeling down for the latches to release the king's horses.

He fled towards the exit when he could no longer catch another breath. He fell twice, tripping on unseen objects that caught his feet. Both times, he heard what he thought was the meowing of a cat.

Unfortunately, he ran into Master Stridler, the stable keeper.

"What happened, boy! Where are the rest?"

"I tried my best, but the flames were too hot."

"What have you done?"

"I...I..."

The castle, awake now, it's bells clanging with urgency. Lots of yelling.

Buckets, pans, water troughs, anything that held water, able-bodied castle inhabitants hauled or carried to help douse flames. People ran everywhere, and so did frightened livestock. A line formed from both the well and the lake.

Soldiers hurried about to bring a semblance of order.

Prince Frederick, the second-born son to King Mikel, up well after his bedtime, witnessed the lightning strike. He watched with interest, the happenings of a serene black night, and how it tumbled into disarray.

Another area of the main keep, where the Queen resided, remained unaffected by the turmoil unfolding down below. Queen Liana's stillborn baby, her first after fourteen long years of infertility, lay wrapped in white silk covering. Her majesty did not want to see the baby once the surgeon delivered the bad news.

This child had not uttered a sound nor made independent movement. The queen looked on at the white shroud seeing the shape of the infant's small form.

Not a tear fell from Queen Liana's eyes.

Her disappointment and her distress kept within her hurt soul. She felt dead herself, laying as if all strength had been taken from her.

Successfully suppressed, the fire became many glowing embers. Boys and young men were tasked with finding the hot spots putting water to them or pounding the heat into nothingness.

To Etan, Master Stridler's form appeared to separate from the slowing movement of the crowd. His overseer's big boots slapped at the mud and puddles, as Etan's heartbeat quickened.

'Maybe I can explain to the king what had happened', he thought to himself. Though, in truth, he was not sure. He struggled against the knotted rope binding his hands behind his back.

The bigger of the two soldiers that guarded him grabbed him up by the collar of the rags he wore and pulled Etan to his feet, almost on his tiptoes. Etan's heartbeat so fast and so hard, he could hardly breathe through the pain his fright cause in his chest.

"This is all your doing boy!" Master Stridler stated, indicating to the soldier, to hand Etan over.

The Soldier shoved Etan toward Master Stridler. He stumbled forward, hitting the wet soil. His face scraped the ground below the mud as he heard a crack and felt an awful pain in his right shoulder. Mud mixed with grainy soil tasted bland and suffocating in his mouth. He pissed himself, and a sob involuntarily rose from him. Both soldiers laughed at Etan as he laid sprayed on the muddy earth.

"Get up, Boy." Master Stridler's anger resonated in the base of his voice, for he alone, not this little son-of-a-mutt, would feel the king's ire at losing seven prized stallions and four finely bred mares. Nine horses had been saved, but more two had to be put down.

Now on his knees, a volley of tears rolled down the young boy's cheek with each remorseful sob. "It wasn't my fault. I...I tried t...to save them... I tried!"

"Get up and answer to your crime." Stridler's anger increased, his eyes hardened with his fury. The king would not be content with this boy's sacrifice, but it must be done.

Stridler thought of how he would justify having only one young boy on duty. An error, he vowed to himself, he would not revisit.

All movement seemed to stop, and the castle grew quiet. Only the wind rustled among the occupants who stood watching. Etan felt the glares of the crowd. Want for sympathy, he rose favoring his injured shoulder. "It w..wasn't my f...f..."

Master Stridler's blade glinted brilliantly off the many torches, as it silently arched striking Etan's young neck. It made a slight thud, but a clean swipe through meat and bone. Etan's fears, forever muted.

Just as Etan's body fell with a thump and his head rolled, a strange sound came through that moonless night to the ears of the castle's quieted occupants.

A baby's cries echoed from the direction of the newly fallen structure of stables. Burnt horse flesh peppered the surrounding air. The castle's exhausted inhabitants turned towards the odd sound and made their sacred signs.

These cries were also heard by the queen. It may have been her unreleased grief, or maybe the queen lost her senses even for that moment. Looking towards her windows, where the echo came in from, she rejoiced, "My baby lives." *'Surely, the gods had finally shined favorably upon me.'*

"Your Highness, those cries are not from your infant," The attending priest chastised softly.

"Then from where? No-one else within this castle is at term."

"We do not know, Your Highness," Lady Lidia answered softly.

The queen looked on at Lady Lidia, her dearest friend, and highest-ranking lady-in-waiting. She reached her hand out, placing it on her dear friend's sleeve. "Find out. I want to know." From nowhere, hope sprang into her heart. "Take two guards with you."

Master Jon got the hounds and ordered them held tightly. Searching the smoldering ruins, the dogs did not pick up a scent.

A wee boy, the same age as Prince Frederick, found the infant. He called to the other searchers, happy that he had been the one to discover her. Looking on as the helpless infant bawled, he carefully picked her up, knocking waning embers and wet wood from her, and held her against his shivering body.

From her, he felt heat emanating, as if she had been on fire. Brice never liked babies. They stunk of piss and shit, demanded attention, and were just nuisances. But this baby's cries pulled at him from within.

She began to quiet as his hold on her felt more secure.

Lead by the castle's friar, the inhabitants of the castle approached and made their sacred signs to ward off evil.

He saw the frightened look on all the faces that he could discern by their torches' lights. He had seen that fear before; when witches were burned. When people whispered about someone being possessed. When mobs formed and did not disband until an unspoken evil was ripped from their midst. "She is just a baby," Brice stated defending the infant. "Helpless soul is all."

"Evil spirit is what she is," Friar Hugh stated stepping back one pace. He did not even want to set eyes on it.

There was no way conceivable that a baby should be found amongst this destruction.

The hounds quieted sitting on their haunches. Brice did not have any love of this friar, nor did the friar for him.

"Put that thing back down. Let the hot timbers take her back down to the hell she came from."

"You will do no such thing," Lady Lidia, stated approaching along with Sir Henning. "Where is your mercy, Friar?" She stepped forward. The lady knew this boy; a kitchen maid's lad, always getting into mischief. "Give her here, Brice."

Brice looked at Lady Lidia suspiciously. "What do you want with her." He took the bottom of his sweater and rolled it around the infant, holding her protectively. Her warmth replaced every bit of cold he felt.

"Her Highness wants to see the babe?"

"There is no mother," Friar Hugh spoke fearful of evil spirits. "She appeared out of nowhere on this darkened night, among embers and burned horses. She is evil. Let her die."

Lidia half listened as she reached down to look at the now peacefully slumbering baby. "Her highness wants to see."

The infant began to bawl again as Lidia took her from Brice.

Not knowing what to do, Brice began kicking at wet charred wood. The further away they walked the more intense the baby's cries became. *She likes me*, he thought to himself. Brice ran up to Lidia, Friar Hugh, and the queen's guards. "Maybe you should give her back to me," Brice offered, feeling the steel edge of the night's cold winds.

The infant's unrelenting crying convinced Lidia to do just that. She carefully transferred the infant back to Brice's little arms. "Careful now. Do not drop her."

Once again, the baby settled into the young boy's arms comfortably, warming him. Brice began to feel a kinship to this strange infant. He felt pride in his role surrounded by the queen's guards and the Lady Lidia. Though he had lived in this castle his whole life, he had only seen the queen in passing or at a distance. Tonight, he, a castle bastard, would finally come face to face with Queen Liana.

Turning onto the hallway that led to the queen's suite, Brice's eyes could not take in all the details. Here the walls were painted with a lot of gold and images of fables and ladies with wings. The wooden floors reflected the light of the sconces. The guards waited outside the queen's grand fancifully painted double doors. Brice could not have imagined this wing of the main keep if he had tried. Inside the queen's suite, Lady Lidia gently escorted him off to the left, to a grand bedchamber painted in pale blue, white, and pink. Brice thought of this place like a would child imagined a fairy tale. If Brice lived a thousand years, he would not soon forget this night. Ms. Otto, a maid, was seen prepping the queen's pillows as the queen sat expectantly, looking toward Brice and Lady Lidia. The surgeon examined something off to a corner.

"Who is this boy?" Queen Liana asked. She did not look at him with kindness and wondered why he held the infant.

"He is a cook's child, Your Majesty."

"Why is he here?" The queen asked more angered.

"The baby seems comforted by him," Lady Lidia quickly answered. "See how she sleeps peacefully in his arms."

The queen's face softened.

"Bring her here, Boy. And be careful you don't drop her."

Brice did not tremble as he thought he would. He slowly made his way to the queen's bedside, not looking at her directly, as he had been taught. Just before he reached the bed Lady Lidia moved in to assist, untangling the infant from his sweater and arms and placed her on the white blanket in the queen's arms. Brice peeked up at the queen's face now. She smiled down at the infant in her arms. Now awake, the baby made movement visible within the cloth that covered her.

The queen was well pleased looking over the infant's body and hearing her tale. She placed the infant at her breast.

"No, your highness, it is an abomination," the friar stated twisting his mouth up at one corner with contempt.

Just then, the queen noticed a small abnormality on Spirit. This she had to keep a secret, for no newborn should be without one. And also, the baby's eyes now appeared green, like her own.